CALLY'S ENTERPRISE

CLAUDIA MILLS is the author of many books for young people, including *The One and Only Cynthia Jane Morton*. She lives with her husband in Takoma Park, Maryland, where she is an editor at the Center for Philosophy and Public Policy at the University of Maryland.

CALLY'S ENTERPRISE

CLAUDIA MILLS

AN AVON CAMELOT BOOK

AVON BOOKS
A division of
The Hearst Corporation
105 Madison Avenue
New York, New York 10016

First Avon Camelot Printing: July 1989

CAMELOT TRADEMARK REG. U.S. PAT. OFF. AND IN OTHER COUNTRIES, MARCA REGISTRADA, HECHO EN U.S.A.

Printed in the U.S.A.

OPM 10 9 8 7 6 5 4 3 2 1

For Katie and Lisa,
Daniel and Rachel,
Jared and Amelia

CALLY'S ENTERPRISE

Chapter 1

Cally lay motionless on the living room couch, her crutches beside her. Under the bright crocheted afghan tucked around her legs, the cast on her left foot loomed enormous, like a square-topped mountain. She pulled herself up to admire it, then flopped back listlessly against the pillows. A pile of text-books lay unopened on the coffee table; the remote control for the television lay untouched on her lap. Cally thought about turning on the TV, but she felt too weak to press the buttons.

Cally Lippincott, Girl Invalid, she thought. She imagined herself as the heroine of a tear-jerker story in a supermarket tabloid. "A once-active eleven-year-old runs and plays no more." Readers would send flowers and telegrams. Even though it was March, a big Christmas party would be held for her, attended by movie stars and famous baseball players, because she was the little girl who might never see another Christmas.

"It's only a broken foot!" Margaret had said, when Cally had asked her, half an hour ago, for a small glass of ginger ale. Cally had used her quavery invalid's voice, and Margaret had snapped, "Honestly, Cally, you'd think you were dying!" But Margaret had brought her the ginger ale, anyway, and some Fig Newtons, too.

Besides, she might die. Her foot might become gangrened, and the decay spread so rapidly that before anyone realized it, like *that*, she'd be gone. Maybe her foot wouldn't heal the way it was supposed to, and that's how they'd find out she had a rare bone disease. A rare *fatal* bone disease. In the meantime, Margaret had better be nice to her, or she'd never be able to forgive herself afterward.

Cally had always wanted to be an invalid. Many of her favorite books featured invalids: Clara in *Heidi*, Colin in *The Secret Garden*, the little lame prince. Most got well in the end, but some didn't. Beth in *Little Women* died, in one of the saddest scenes Cally had ever read. Cally could quote it by heart: Those who loved her "smiled through their tears and thanked God that Beth was well at last." Let that be a lesson to Margaret, or one of these days she might be smiling through her tears and thanking God that Cally was "well at last."

It wasn't the kind of ambition she mentioned to her parents. They wanted her to be a brain surgeon, or a partner in a top law firm, or an investment banker. But that was the beauty of being an invalid: You didn't have to be any of those things other people wanted you to be. Nobody would care what your grades were, or whether you won the gymnastics meet, or got the biggest part in the ballet, or played the hardest piece in the piano recital. You wouldn't have to dash from lesson to lesson, never wasting a minute. You could do whatever *you* wanted to do—well, so long as it didn't involve moving around very much.

Cally adjusted her pillow. She could hardly remember being home after school. On Mondays and Wednesdays she had gymnastics, with another workout on Saturday afternoons; on Tuesdays and Thursdays she had ballet. Fridays were set aside for her piano lessons. But now she couldn't possibly do ballet and gymnastics. So until her cast came off in six weeks, she'd gained five free afternoons.

"Do you want some more ginger ale?" Margaret asked from the doorway.

"Maybe a little bit," Cally whispered feebly.

Margaret strode over to the couch. With her ruddy cheeks and tousled short curls, no one looked less like an invalid than Margaret did. She peered down at Cally. "Does your foot hurt?"

It did, now that Cally thought about it. She nodded, concentrating on looking pale and helpless. Luckily she had the white, freckled complexion to match her red hair.

"Faker," Margaret said.

In a minute she returned with Cally's glass, brimful of ginger ale.

"How's Steven?" Cally asked. Steven was her almost-two-year-old brother, and the main reason Margaret lived with them. In exchange for looking after Steven, Margaret, a junior at the university, got free room and board at the Lippincotts'.

"He's fine. Why?"

"Well, I mean, does he feel terrible? About my foot? Because if he hadn't left the vacuum cleaner on the stairs this morning, I wouldn't have tripped, and I wouldn't have broken my foot, and I'd be at the gymnastics meet right now, and I'd probably be getting a medal."

"Somehow I don't think he's made those connections."

"I don't want him to be scarred for life, or anything."

"Do you know what your problem is?" Margaret asked.

Before Cally could plunge into one of her lists, Margaret answered for her. "You need to lighten up. Look on the bright side. Steven's not going to be scarred for life. You're not going to die of a broken foot. By tomorrow you're even going to be getting your own ginger ale."

"You call that looking on the bright side?" Cally demanded. "Gee, thanks a lot."

"Any time, pardner. Listen, I'm taking Stevie outside for a while, to burn off some energy before dinner. Why don't you do some homework?"

Cally shook her head.

"Or read a book. Or watch some TV."

Cally wasn't going to waste the first of her glorious free afternoons doing anything so ordinary. "I'll think of something."

"Have fun," Margaret said.

Steven came to kiss her before he went outside. "Cally go boom," he said. "Vacuum go boom." The two disasters were on a par, as far as Steven was concerned.

"Boom yourself," Cally said, summoning the last of her strength to give him a hug.

The house was very quiet once the door banged shut behind Steven and Margaret. No wonderful idea had occurred to Cally yet, so she flipped on the TV, after all. She clicked around the dial, past soap operas and a black-and-white movie, to "Sesame Street." Steven was allowed to watch "Sesame Street" once in a while, because it was educational. But usually her parents preferred Margaret to play counting games with him and do vocabulary drill. Steven could count to sixteen, her parents liked to tell their friends. The next-door neighbors had a daughter two weeks older than Steven, who could only count to twelve. However, Amy had crawled and walked ahead of Steven, a dark period in Lippincott family history. Amy also had more teeth.

"So, Amy is ahead on teeth, Steven is ahead on brains," Mr. Lippincott would say, trying to sound fair-minded and impartial.

On "Sesame Street" two of the puppet characters—Cally didn't know their names—were tap-dancing around their beds, singing a catchy tune that made Cally's toes twitch. But she felt guilty watching TV in the middle of the day, so she switched it off and stared at her foot again.

There must be something that she felt like doing. Cally almost opened her science book. They were having a test in science the day after tomorrow, and if Cally got an A on the test, she'd be guaranteed an A for the marking period. If her mother were home, she'd make sure Cally was busy reviewing. But her mother was still at the university, teaching her graduate economics seminar. And Cally had a feeling that studying science would make her foot hurt. Just the thought of studying made it tingle in a painful way.

There was always reading. Cally had read a lot of books in fifth grade, because the fifth-grade teacher had given extra credit for book reports. But the sixth-grade English teacher didn't want to grade additional papers, so Cally had hardly read a book since September. Instead, she had used the time for practicing the piano. Mrs. Randolph had told Cally's parents that Cally was one of her most promising piano students. With a broken foot she'd still be able to practice—not with the pedals, of course. But even though she liked the piano best of all her after-school activities, she didn't feel like practicing right now, either. Cally could hardly believe that after waiting so long to have free time, she couldn't think of a thing to do with it.

The doorbell rang. Cally jumped. She was allowed to answer the door, so long as she kept the chain latched and didn't let any strangers come inside. But she didn't feel like hobbling across the room on her crutches. She lay very still, waiting for the caller to go away. Instead the doorbell rang again, a long, insistent peal. Whoever it was banged the brass knocker, too, for good measure.

Maybe Margaret had forgotten her key. The bell sounded a third time. Cally eased herself into a sitting position and then stood up awkwardly, tucking a crutch under each arm. It took her a long time to maneuver across the room, and her shoulders ached.

When she opened the door a crack, she saw a boy her own age, with piercing blue eyes and a monkeylike grin. He wore faded blue jeans and a neatly pressed plaid shirt. A shiny metal change dispenser hung from his belt.

"Hi, I'm Chuck Foster, and I'm selling subscriptions to the *County Times*. I've sold eighty-seven subscriptions already. So, how about it, do I hear eighty-eight?"

"How much does it cost?" Cally asked, just to be polite. She knew her parents didn't want to subscribe to any more newspapers.

"Just pennies a week," Chuck said. "And we deliver to your door in all weather. Like, if you wake up and it's a rainy, miserable day and you want to sit around reading the *County Times* in your bathrobe? Well, you don't have to go out and get it. You look out your front door, and there it is."

He sounded so cheerful and energetic that Cally hated to disappoint him. "My parents aren't home. But I know they

6

wouldn't buy one. They never buy anything door-to-door."

"What about you? Do you have any money? It's just ninety cents a week. All you need for our introductory offer is an eight-week commitment."

"Well, I have to go check. Only it's upstairs and I don't know if I can walk that far."

Since it wasn't anyone scary, Cally undid the chain.

"Hey, what happened to you?" Chuck asked, catching sight of her crutches.

"I broke my foot." Cally wiggled her cast proudly. For a few minutes she had forgotten she was an invalid, looking forward to an early grave. But with Chuck's admiring glance it all came back to her.

"You wait right here," Chuck said soothingly. "I'll go get your money. Just tell me where it is."

Cally hesitated. She couldn't have a strange boy poking through her bureau drawers. But Chuck had such an impish smile, and he wanted to sell that subscription so much. Cally didn't think she had ever wanted anything that way. Not enough to knock on strangers' doors for it.

"I'm sorry," she said. "But I can't."

"That's all right," Chuck said. "I'll come back tomorrow, and you can give me the money then."

"Well, if I have it."

"So it's a deal!" He put out his hand, and Cally found herself shaking it.

"How come you want to sell papers so much?" she asked, curious. "Is it for a project at school?"

"Are you kidding? No, it's for a contest. If I sell more than anyone else I win a trip to Ocean City."

"Your parents must really want you to win."

7

Chuck grinned. "Actually, they've had about all they can take of the *County.Times* by now. But you'd better believe that *I* want to win. I want it so bad I can taste it."

"Do you think you will?"

"Sure I do. You have to believe in yourself, right?" Chuck's face suddenly lit up. "Listen, have I got an idea! How about you come to work for me? I'll give you half the profits, only all the subscriptions will count toward my trip to Ocean City. What do you say?"

Cally couldn't have been more surprised if Chuck had asked her to run away and join the circus. But she felt tempted in spite of herself. It would be something to do, and she *had* been looking for something to do.

"What about my cast? I can't walk very well."

Chuck's face fell, but only for an instant. "Okay, we won't start until tomorrow. I'll bring my wagon, and I'll pull you most of the way. You'll only have to walk a few steps at each house. You can do that, can't you? You have a whole day to practice."

"I don't know if my parents—"

"Parents love this kind of thing. Mine bought two subscriptions right off the bat. Yours will, too, now that you're on board. What did you say your name was?"

"Cally, but—"

"Cally, you and I have our fortunes made." He was backing down the path. "Wear pigtails!" he called from the road. He yanked at two imaginary pigtails growing straight out of the sides of his head. "With bows!"

Exhausted, Cally shut the door and put the lock in place. Chuck's relentless energy had worn her out more than an hour of backflips in gymnastics. She couldn't believe he worked so hard selling newspapers, not because he had to do it for a project at school, or because his parents would be disappointed if he didn't, but just because he wanted to. Chuck would never have a whole free afternoon to himself and not know what to do with it. Apparently Chuck got ideas faster than a pig could blink, as Cally's grandfather used to say. But he had no business assuming willy-nilly that other people would go along with them. Cally didn't know if she wanted to be his partner or not.

She clumped back to the couch in time to remember: She was an invalid. She might never walk again. She might never see another spring. Wearily she sank back on the cushions and arranged the afghan over her throbbing leg.

In the kitchen she heard Margaret and Steven, back from their walk, laughing and talking.

"Margaret?" she called, her voice in full quaver. "Could you bring me a little more ginger ale?"

Chapter 2

At the sound of her mother's Volvo purring into the driveway, Cally opened her science book to the chapter on electricity. She studied the diagram of a dry cell battery. Mr. Abdul, the science teacher, often put a diagram on his tests for the students to label. It was the easiest kind of question if you had memorized the book, the hardest if you hadn't. But Cally was a whiz at memorization.

"Electrons are negative, protons are positive," she repeated under her breath. The secret to memorizing was to find little clues to hold on to. Here the clue was obvious: *Protons* and *positive* both began with a *p*.

"Cally! How's your foot?" Her mother hurried across the living room and perched on the arm of the couch. Two small worry lines deepened between her auburn eyebrows.

"It's fine," Cally said. "It doesn't hurt at all. Really."

"Fine!" Mrs. Lippincott said, staring down at Cally's cast in despair. "I'd hardly say it was fine! You poor thing. You must have been terribly disappointed to miss the meet. And now, to miss six whole weeks of gymnastics workouts—and ballet, too."

"Oh, I'll catch up in no time," Cally said. Her mother took everything so hard that Cally was forced to sound hearty. The little lame princess vanished, and a future Olympic champion appeared in her place.

"What did you do all afternoon?"

I got a job selling newspaper subscriptions door-to-door. Do you want to buy one? Cally thought about saying, but didn't. She pointed to her science book.

The worry lines between her mother's eyebrows smoothed away. "Well, this cloud may turn out to have a silver lining yet. This could be the marking period when you come home with straight A's. Did you work on your careers project for social studies?"

"A little bit," Cally lied.

"It's due on Friday, right? After dinner we'll sit down together and see if we can finish it off."

"What's for dinner?"

"I picked up some carry-out from Hunan Village. It'll just be the four of us. Your dad's plane doesn't get in until nine-thirty." Mr. Lippincott was an important lawyer who defended the kind of criminals who made the six o'clock news. For the past three days he had been at a conference in Toronto.

"Does he know about my foot?"

"When I called him from the hospital this morning, he was in a meeting. But he reached me at the office this afternoon. You know how your father is. Nothing fazes him. I'm in tears telling him about it, and he says he wants to be the first one to autograph your cast! But I'm sure he's as upset as we all are that you lost your chance at the meet this afternoon."

The more her mother talked about the gymnastics meet, the better Cally felt about having missed it. Because she might have come home with a medal if she hadn't broken her foot. But, then again, she might not.

Steven ran into the living room, dragging the entire vacuum cleaner behind him. "Noise, noise!" he pleaded, hoping Margaret would relent and plug it in.

"Maybe later," Margaret said, bringing up the rear in the procession.

Mrs. Lippincott looked worried again. "I'm not sure that's the best toy for him to be playing with." She glanced meaningfully at Cally's cast.

"Oh, Cally could have tripped on anything," Margaret said. "If it hadn't been the vacuum cleaner, it would have been something else."

"But what's he learning from the vacuum cleaner?"

"He's learning how to vacuum. Here, Stevie." Margaret stooped down and plugged the cord into the nearest socket. Then she nudged the on button with her bare foot. As the machine gave its mighty roar, Steven sprang into action with all his might. Back and forth he went over the same small patch of carpet, a tiny figure vacuuming with a singleminded ferocity that reduced Cally and her mother to helpless laughter.

Margaret's toe reached for the off button. The room was suddenly quiet.

"More noise?" Steven asked hopefully.

"The vacuum cleaner has to rest now," Margaret said, "while we have dinner."

"That's right," Mrs. Lippincott said, wiping tears of laughter from her eyes. "We should eat before it gets cold."

Hunan Village had the best Chinese food in the suburbs,

according to Cally's parents, and Cally's parents knew where to get the best of everything: the best homemade pasta, the freshest produce, the zestiest seafood salad. Certainly the carry-out from Hunan Village was delicious—hot and sour soup that brought Cally's mouth alive, spicy Szechuan chicken, dark duck meat in a rich sauce. Steven still ate with a spoon—helped along by fingers—but Cally and her mother managed expertly with chopsticks. To Mr. and Mrs. Lippincott's great embarrassment, Margaret insisted on eating Chinese food, even in public, with a fork.

"It tastes the same either way," Margaret had said, perplexed that it should matter to the Lippincotts which utensil she used. But showing yourself to be knowledgeable about food was very important to Cally's parents. Cally sometimes thought their idea of hell would be having to eat Chinese food with a fork, in front of people who thought they didn't know any better. Or, worse, she added wickedly, being caught eating chow mein. They considered chow mein a fake, Americanized version of Chinese food. Eating chow mein with a fork—that would be the end of Cally's parents.

"What are you grinning about?" Mrs. Lippincott asked warily.

"Nothing," Cally said. "Steven with the vacuum cleaner."

Steven perked up. "Noise?"

"No!" the others said together.

Usually Cally cleared the table and loaded the dishwasher, but in honor of her broken foot her mother did it instead. "Go get your careers project organized," Mrs. Lippincott told her. "This will just take a minute."

Cally found the stack of papers for her project buried

13

under another pile on the big worktable in the den. She looked through them without interest. As part of a six-week social studies unit on careers, the sixth-graders had taken aptitude tests, visited various workplaces on field trips, and seen films showing a day in the life of a doctor, a museum director, and a congressman. The centerpiece of the unit was an individual project on some particular career of your choice.

As soon as Cally's parents had heard about the assignment, they had devoted themselves to finding just the right career for her to write about. Not computers, the obvious first choice. It was sure to be the first choice of everyone else, as well. They rejected medicine on similar grounds.

Cally had a few ideas herself, but she knew without asking that they weren't appropriate for her school project. So far her only ambitions were to grow up to be a candy store owner, an ice cream store owner, or an invalid.

"I have it!" her father had said. "An aerodynamics engineer!"

"What's that?" Cally had asked, her heart sinking.

"An engineer who measures lift and drag forces acting on moving vehicles."

Cally still didn't know what it was, or, even less, why anyone would want to *be* it.

"Like my brother Chip," her father had continued. "Chip'll be delighted to talk to you, take you through the plant—I'll give him a call first thing in the morning."

So that was that. Cally's father had been so enthusiastic about his brainstorm that Cally hadn't had the heart to oppose him. If it meant so much to her parents that she do her report on aerodynamics engineering, aerodynamics engineering it would be.

Uncle Chip was eager to help, but as it turned out, he wasn't very good at explaining what he did for a living.

"Look," he had told Cally. "Air is a viscous fluid, so any object moving through it experiences a drag. An aerodynamics engineer tries to reduce that drag."

"Air is a what? A vis-vis . . ."

"*Viscous.* V-i-s-c-o-u-s. A viscous fluid. You know, sticky, cohesive."

Cally had written it down. It sounded awful. If air was a viscous fluid, she didn't know if she wanted to breathe it.

Now the project was almost done. Her father had taken photographs of various aircraft and the enormous wind tunnel where Uncle Chip helped to test them. Her mother had edited Cally's report and typed it on her personal computer. Tonight they were going to print out the final draft and assemble the whole thing in a special plastic folder. If Cally didn't get an A on this one, it wouldn't be because her parents hadn't tried.

Suddenly, for no reason, she thought of Chuck Foster. If *he* was doing a careers project, what would it be on? She had a feeling he wouldn't let his parents pick a topic for him. He'd have so many ideas of his own, and he'd be so set on them, that nobody else's would stand a chance.

"Okay," her mother said, coming up behind her. "Why don't you work on the captions for Daddy's photos while I warm up the printer. Actually I think he already wrote captions on the back of each one. So just copy them neatly on these little tags."

Cally picked up the first photo, turned it over, and dutifully copied: "Cross-sections of proposed models are often tested in wind tunnels." She sighed.

Her mother looked over at her anxiously. She hated when Cally moped. "We're on the home stretch now," Mrs. Lippincott said. "We'll be done before you know it."

Cally flashed what she hoped was a toothy Olympic champion grin and began copying the next caption: "Models are tested in water, as well. Smoke or colored dye is used to trace the flow of fluid around the surface."

An hour later the project was done, safely tucked between the covers of its plastic jacket. Cally felt as if an enormous weight had been lifted from her heart.

For the first time all day it occurred to her to be curious about how the rest of the girls had done at the gymnastics meet. Her best friend, Heather, answered the telephone on the second ring. Before Cally could ask any questions, Heather squealed, "I came in second!"

"I told you you'd do great. What about Ashley?"

"Oh, Cally, it was awful, it was so *sad*," Heather said happily. "She fell off the balance beam. *Fell off!* She didn't get hurt or anything, but she started crying, right in front of everybody, and she didn't finish her routine."

"Poor Ashley!" Cally said. There was a long pause, and both girls burst out laughing. Cally knew it was mean to laugh, but Ashley bragged about herself so tirelessly that it was hard not to enjoy her fleeting moments of disgrace.

"But your foot," Heather remembered. "Are you okay? Will you be in school tomorrow? When can you come back to ballet?"

"Not for six weeks."

Heather gasped.

"But I'll be in school tomorrow. I finished my careers project tonight, before I called."

"We did mine yesterday." Heather's parents had made her do her project on neurosurgery. "Six weeks! What will you do?"

"Nothing, I guess." She lowered her voice. "I met a boy."

"A *boy*? At the hospital?"

"No, selling something door-to-door."

"And?"

"He's cute. Sort of. I mean, not like Scott or Justin. He's— different."

"Where does he go to school? Are you going to see him again?"

"I don't know. Maybe." Cally still wasn't sure she wanted to be Chuck's sales partner. But it might be fun to get to know him better. There was something about his bright blue eyes and boundless enthusiasm that made her like him in spite of his pushiness. "I think so," she said.

Chapter 3

By three o'clock the next afternoon Cally was heartily sick of her cast and crutches, and couldn't remember why she had ever wanted to be an invalid. It had been fun making a grand entrance into homeroom, with everyone staring as Mr. Allen helped her to her seat. Justin Levine, the most popular boy in the sixth grade, gallantly carried Cally's books to first-period science class, and at lunch admiration of Cally's cast edged out a discussion of yesterday's gymnastics meet. All this attention was new and pleasant, and Cally never minded having a fuss made over her.

But as the day wore on the fuss lessened. Cally's broken foot began to throb; her good foot rebelled against doing the work of both feet; her armpits became sore and strained from the pressure of the crutches against them. Her shoulders were stiff. Tiny hammers pounded inside her head.

"How do you feel?" Margaret asked, when she picked Cally up after school.

"Awful," Cally said. "If you really want to know, it was torture. Agony. I am in terrible, excruciating pain."

"Okay, okay, I get the general picture," Margaret said, tossing Cally's crutches into the cluttered backseat of her ancient VW. "Don't worry, it'll be better tomorrow. Your muscles'll get used to it."

Cally could picture Margaret striding through a battlefield, smiling gaily at the wounded soldiers writhing all around her. *Cheer up*, Margaret would tell them. *Either you'll live or you won't. What's there to boo-hoo about?*

"I think it'll be *much worse* tomorrow," Cally said.

"Maybe when we get home you should take a nap until dinner," Margaret suggested.

"I can't."

Margaret shot Cally a quizzical glance.

"I mean, someone might stop by."

"Like who?"

"Nobody." For all Cally knew, Chuck might not even come.

"Suit yourself," Margaret said agreeably.

At home Cally settled herself once more on the couch and closed her eyes. She hoped Chuck wouldn't come, she really did. She was more tired than she had ever been in her life.

At a quarter past three the doorbell chimed.

"I'll get it!" Cally shouted. She yanked her crutches into place and swung across the living room, getting to the door just as the bell rang a second time. When she opened it, there was Chuck, his eyes even bluer and his grin broader than Cally had remembered. Behind him he pulled a dented, rusty, once-red wagon.

"Where are the pigtails?" he demanded.

"Well—I'm not sure I can come. Today was my first day back at school and I'm really tired."

"Of course you're coming. I brought the wagon just for you. Did you remember your money? Seven dollars and twenty cents."

Actually she had gotten it ready for him that morning. She had decided that if she didn't end up being his assistant, at least she could help him out by giving him one more subscription.

"Here it is." Cally took an envelope from the shallow drawer in the little carved table that stood next to the door. Quickly Chuck counted it, snapping each bill crisply, the way tellers at the bank did.

"Look, I'll make the pigtails," Chuck said, when he had counted the money a second time. "I even brought ribbons, see? Swiped 'em from my sisters, in case you didn't have any."

"I told you, I don't think—"

But the next thing Cally knew, Chuck had steered her into the living room and eased her back onto the couch. Sitting beside her, he whipped a small plastic comb from his pocket and began deftly gathering her hair into two cascading pigtails.

"I have three little sisters," he explained. "I could make pigtails in my sleep."

He tied a gigantic bow on each one. "Customers like pigtails. They go for the perky look." He helped Cally over to the brass-framed mirror that hung over the Lippincotts' fireplace. "Look at that."

Cally stared at her reflection. The golden red pigtails were perky, all right.

In the mirror she saw Margaret coming up behind them. Reluctantly she made the introductions, avoiding Margaret's amused eyes.

"Um—Margaret, this is Chuck Foster."

"Cally's going to be helping me sell newspapers door-to-door," Chuck told Margaret. "If I sell the most I win a trip to Ocean City. Would you like to be her first customer? The cost is just pennies a day."

"Like how many pennies?"

"Seven dollars and twenty cents for eight weeks. Do it for Cally."

Margaret grinned. "I'm a soft touch. Put me down for one. And you"—she looked at Cally—"seem to have recovered rather quickly. Better be home by the time your mother gets here. Okay?"

"Okay," Cally said, trying to pinpoint the exact moment at which it had become too late to back out. Probably when she had first opened the door for Chuck yesterday afternoon.

"Can you get the money now?" Chuck asked Margaret politely. "Management doesn't like me to extend credit."

"Sure, sure." Margaret left to get it, and Chuck winked at Cally. "We're on, Cally-o. We are the team that can't be beat."

Once outside, Cally tried to make herself comfortable in Chuck's wagon, but there was no good place to put her broken foot until Chuck thought of propping it on a crutch extending out behind the wagon. She held on tightly as Chuck hurried down the bumpy sidewalk, past forsythia in bloom and lawns bordered by early-blooming daffodils.

Two blocks later he stopped. "Out you go," he said, offering Cally his hand. "I'll take one side of the street, you take the other."

"But I thought we were going to go together."

"No, we'll cover twice as much territory this way."

Cally fought back a wave of panic. She would never have let herself be talked into this if she had thought she'd have to knock on the door of complete strangers, all by herself, and ask them to buy something. What would she say? She hadn't practiced; she had no speech ready. She remembered something about "pennies a day" from Chuck's opening spiel, but that was all. What if they asked questions and she didn't know the answers? Was the County Times a morning or an afternoon paper? Did it have any comics? She didn't know a thing about it. She had never even heard of the County Times until Chuck Foster had tried to sell it to her hardly twenty-four hours ago.

"I can't," Cally said, panic turning to anger. "You never said anything about doing it this way. We were supposed to be a team. You'd do the talking, and I'd—look perky."

"But think how much faster it'll be if we can do two houses at once. You're not being logical, Cally."

"You're not being logical. First you say one thing, then you say the complete opposite."

"But doesn't this make more sense?" Chuck kicked at a loose patch of gravel with the worn tip of his sneaker. Suddenly his face brightened with a new idea. "You're not scared, are you, Cally?"

"Of course not," Cally said hotly, but she could feel her face giving her away.

"Because you'll be great at it. You're so pretty, and with the pigtails—believe me, you're a natural."

Cally didn't let herself react to Chuck's saying she was pretty. "But what should I say? I don't know what to say."

Chuck flung out his arms wide. "Say anything! Tell them about my prize trip. Tell them what a bargain the County Times is, just pennies a day, delivered to their door in all weather. The up-and-coming paper! The most classified ads in the region! That gets lots of people."

"Is that true, though?" Cally asked suspiciously. "That it has the most classified ads in the region?" She wasn't sure she trusted anyone who talked as fast as Chuck did.

"A good salesman doesn't lie," Chuck said, suddenly serious. "Stretches the truth, maybe—emphasizes some facts and forgets to mention others. For example, I wouldn't mention the fact that, judged strictly as a newspaper, the *County Times* stinks. But most classified ads? That's true. Pennies a day? That's true, too. So what do you say? Go get 'em, tiger?"

Cally gave up. "I'll *try*."

Chuck beamed. "Atta girl, Cally! Knock 'em dead! Here, I got you your own money purse, and here's the pad where you write down their names and addresses. I've numbered up to fifty for you, to save you time later."

Fifty, Cally thought. She'd be lucky to get one.

She felt more and more miserable as Chuck stuffed the change purse and subscription pad into a large canvas pouch—which he had also provided—and tied it securely around her waist. The bow on one of her pigtails had begun to droop, so Chuck retied it for her. Too soon the moment came for Cally to launch her career in sales.

Chuck had already started up the front walk of his first house. He turned back once to give Cally a big wave and an encouraging smile. She clumped her way painfully up to a large gray-painted brick house and stood for a long moment on the front stoop. Finally she made herself ring the bell.

Under her breath she began counting to ten. When she reached ten she could run—or, rather, hobble—away. But on the count of eight, a grandfatherly man opened the door.

The man looked at Cally as if he expected her to say something. Heather's father often answered the telephone (very rudely, in Cally's opinion) by barking, "It's your dime, start talking." By this he meant that if you were the person who had made the call, presumably you had something to say and you should say it. But although Cally had rung this man's doorbell, she couldn't think of a thing to say to him.

"Are you selling something?" the man asked, to help her along. "Candy? Raffle tickets?"

"Newspaper subscriptions," Cally whispered.

"To which newspaper?"

"The *County Times*."

"How much is it?"

"Seven dollars and twenty cents."

"For how many weeks?"

"Eight."

"The *County Times*. It's not much of a paper, but they do have a lot of classified ads. I'll take it."

It had all happened so quickly. "Thank you," Cally managed to squeak.

"Should I pay you now?"

"I think so. I mean, yes."

The man pulled a ten-dollar bill from his wallet. "Do you have change for this? Wait, I have it right here." He offered her a five, two ones, and four nickels. Awkwardly, she propped one crutch against the side of the house and took the money with her free hand.

"Thank you," she said again. She reached for her crutch to go.

"Don't you need to take down my name and address?"

Of course she did. Cally fumbled in her canvas pouch for the subscription pad and one of Chuck's freshly sharpened pencils.

"You're going to have trouble trying to write with one hand," the man said. "Here, let me do it." He printed his name and address neatly on the top of the first numbered page.

"Well, good day." He tucked the pad and pencil back into Cally's pouch, handed her her crutch, lifted his hand in good-bye, and shut the front door.

Numbly, Cally headed back to the street. Returning from his first customer, Chuck gave the thumbs-up sign, then caught sight of Cally's face. "No luck? Don't worry. You'll get the hang of it. And some of these people have actually read the *County Times*. It's ten to one *they* aren't going to buy it."

"I think I sold one," Cally said faintly. Chuck's expression changed abruptly from one of condolence to one of congratulation. "But he did all the talking, so it doesn't really count."

"Did you get the money?" Chuck asked. Cally nodded. "Then it counts."

"But—"

"No buts. You've made your first sale!"

Cally wouldn't say she had *made* a sale. A sale had *happened* to her, while she had stood there, tongue-tied, speaking only when spoken to. But she undeniably had seven dollars and twenty cents more than she had had five minutes before.

"Keep up the good work!" Chuck called over his shoulder as he started up the second walk. Cally's heart sank. One sale seemed enough for the afternoon. It seemed enough for the rest of her life.

No one was home at Cally's second house. Chuck had said that after school wasn't the best time for door-to-door selling, since most people were at work. Cally made a note on her pad to try that house again on Saturday, the way Chuck had told her to. If she lasted till Saturday.

A slim woman wearing a dancer's leotard and tights came to the door at the next house. She must have had an extremely loud doorbell to hear it over the aerobics videotape blaring in the background. The woman continued to bob in time to the music as she waited for Cally to speak her piece.

Apparently no one was going to do her work for her this time, so Cally began. "I'm selling subscriptions to the *County Times* and—"

"I'm sorry, we're not interested," the aerobics dancer said, and shut the door.

Just like that? Cally thought. She hadn't even had a chance to explain about Chuck's prize or the classified ads or anything. Through the porch window she could see the woman leaping and stretching as if her life depended on keeping up with the video instructor. How could someone be that interested in aerobics and not one bit interested in the *County Times*?

"Your job is to *make* them interested," Chuck said, when she reported back.

"But she shut the door so fast."

"Next time get your foot in it first." Chuck looked down at Cally's cast. "Maybe that's not such a good idea. Just talk faster, that's all."

When the next customer answered the bell, Cally burst into her speech, this time starting with her best material. That way if the door slammed shut partway through, at least she'd have said most of what she wanted to say.

"Did you know that the *County Times* has more classified ads than any other paper in the region?" she asked. "And for just pennies a day you can have it delivered to your doorstep."

"I do look at ads for yard sales," the woman said slowly, thinking it over.

"The *County Times* has the most of anybody. We deliver to your door in all weather, too. Rain, shine, snow, sleet, hail." Cally tried to think if there were any other kinds of weather. "Fog. Tornadoes."

"What the heck, I'll take one. If I get enough bargains at yard sales, it'll pay for itself."

"You won't be sorry," Cally said joyfully. Another seven dollars and twenty cents. Another subscription toward the grand prize.

By the end of the afternoon she had sold six more. Chuck had sold nine. As he pulled her home in the little red wagon, Chuck sang, "Ocean City, Here I Come!" At first Cally didn't sing. She still didn't like the fact that Chuck had dragooned her into coming along with him. But irritation with Chuck battled with an odd jubilation. She, Cally Lippincott, had sold eight subscriptions, all by herself! Selling newspapers with Chuck had been undeniably fun, more fun than she could remember. Her money purse jingled merrily, and after a chorus or two she found herself joining in, singing almost as loudly as Chuck did, "Ocean City, Here We Come!"

Chapter 4

Cally loved when both her parents were home for dinner. Often her father had to stay late at the law firm or was traveling on business; her mother gave several talks a semester at universities around the country, and sometimes in Europe, too. It wasn't unusual for a whole week to go by without one regular family dinner.

But Cally was impressed at how important her parents were. Her mother might someday win the Nobel Prize in economics. Mrs. Lippincott laughed when Cally said that, but Cally took the possibility seriously. Every year some economist won the Nobel Prize. Why shouldn't it be her mother? If her mother had been a dentist or a librarian, there wouldn't have been any chance at all of winning a Nobel Prize, since there was no Nobel Prize for dentistry or librarianship. But for economics there certainly was, and once a year Cally waited eagerly for the award to be announced. So far it had always gone to somebody else.

Cally was in awe of her father because he had met real-live murderers. He had lunch sometimes with murderers, the way Cally had lunch with Ashley and Heather. "Excuse me," he'd say to the murderer, "would you please pass the catsup?" And the murderer would say, "No trouble at all," and hand the catsup bottle to her father as politely as could be. Cally felt sorry for people whose parents could never win a Nobel Prize or make small talk with hardened killers.

That night the whole family was home for dinner. Mr. and Mrs. Lippincott had to work late, so Margaret had made the meal—one of Cally's favorites, shrimp creole. Left on her own, Margaret would just open a can of something, but Cally's parents had bought her a step-by-step gourmet cook-book for the family dinners. So even if Margaret didn't eat Chinese food with chopsticks, at least she could make half a dozen recipes with fancy names.

"What did you do after school today?" her mother asked Cally, reaching over to butter a slice of bread for Steven. "Did you take a nap, or did you review some more for your science test?"

"Um—well, neither, really."

"Steven, if you throw it, I won't give you another one. Well, I'm sure you had a lot of other homework, too."

Cally could have left it at that, but they'd find out about her job sooner or later. She might as well get it over with. "I have this new friend, Chuck, and he's selling subscriptions door-to-door, for this newspaper, and I sort of helped." The news spurted out of her. "Guess how many subscriptions I sold today? Eight! All by myself. Almost sixty dollars' worth."

Steven's bread landed, butter side down, on the floor, but Cally's mother didn't notice. "Oh, Cally, I'm sure Doctor Romano would be very upset if he had any idea. And your science test. Margaret, did you know about this?"

"He was a nice kid," Margaret said, unruffled as usual. "He brought a wagon with him so Cally wouldn't have to walk very far. And I figured it's not as if she usually does home-work in the afternoons, anyway. I figured this was instead of gymnastics or ballet."

"Yes, but those are—well, they're very different."

"What newspaper?" Mr. Lippincott asked.

"The *County Times*. It's just pennies a day, delivered to your door in all weather. The most classified ads in the region. And all the high school sports scores every week." Cally had added this new fact to her sales spiel.

Her father grinned. "Honey, I think we should subscribe. This sounds like one bargain we can't pass up."

"Be serious," Mrs. Lippincott said. "Look at her. She's obvi-ously exhausted, and she still has that test to study for this evening."

Cally sat up straighter and tried to look hale and hearty. For good measure, she flashed the Olympic champion smile, with lots of teeth.

Cally's father buttered a second slice of bread for Steven. He never took things as hard as Cally's mother did. Eating lunch so often with murderers had prepared him for any-thing.

"What got you interested in selling papers?" he asked. "Allowance too small?"

"No, it's a contest. If Chuck sells more than anyone else, he wins a trip. To Ocean City."

"What about you? What do you get?"

"Chuck said he'd give me half the money. And it's—I don't know—it's fun."

"You're sure it won't interfere with your schoolwork?"

"*And* your piano lessons," Mrs. Lippincott put in, giving

her husband an exasperated look. "And, remember, Gerry, she's been getting Bs in science, and in math, too. Some extra study time wouldn't hurt her one bit."

"Suppose we compromise. You have five more free afternoons now, till your cast comes off. How about spending two on science and math in exchange for three on your sales contest?

"Look," Mr. Lippincott added, since Cally's mother didn't seem very pleased with the arrangement, "it's not as if she were going to make a career out of it."

No, Cally didn't want to make a career out of door-to-door sales. But she'd have to say that so far she liked newspaper sales a thousand times more than she would ever like aerodynamics engineering.

Despite her mother's fretting, Cally sailed through the science test first period Friday morning. Speedily she labeled all the parts of a dry cell battery and filled in the blanks in the short-answer questions. "The electrical charge on a proton is _____." Positive!

At lunch, Cally sat with Ashley and Heather.

"I can't believe it," Ashley said. "I can't believe Miss Landsburg picked me for the biggest part in the spring ballet. I mean, I thought maybe I had heard wrong or something. But she said it twice, so then I knew it was really true."

Ashley wound her long, flaxen hair around her finger dreamily as she talked. Heather, who had tried out for the same part, stared down at her plate and said nothing.

"Heather's the lucky one," Ashley went on. "She has an itty-bitty part where no one'll ever know or care if she messes up. And of course you're out of everything, Cally. But with a part as big as mine, everyone will be watching me every minute, so if I make one mistake . . ." She shivered with joy at her own importance.

"Look at it this way," Cally said. "Whatever happens, it can't be as bad as falling off the balance beam at the gymnastics meet, and you lived through that."

Ashley glared at Cally, but Cally smiled back at her sweetly.

"Anyway," Ashley said, "whatever happens at the ballet won't matter, since I'm going to be leaving for camp as soon as school gets out for summer. I found out yesterday which camp I'm going to."

She waited for the other girls to ask, but neither did.

"Camp Danforth. It's for the gifted and talented. You have to take a test to get in. The brochure said it's more selective than the Ivy League. They only take one person for every five who apply."

"Did they write you a letter telling you you got in?" Heather asked casually, and then Cally knew that Heather had applied to Camp Danforth, too, and hadn't heard anything yet.

"Uh-huh. You can tell by the envelope whether it's good news or bad. Good news is a fat envelope, because then they stick a whole bunch of other forms in with it. You know, for your camp physical and everything. Bad news is a thin letter with just one sentence: 'Forget it!'" Ashley laughed shrilly. "I think they mail the yeses first, and then the nos."

Cally saw Heather's eyes glistening with tears. She felt like telling Ashley to stop bragging. *It makes other people feel bad when you brag so much*, she imagined herself saying. But Cally knew that she would never be able to open her mouth and have the words come out, just like that. It would be like telling Ashley she had bad breath or ring-around-the-collar, the kind of thing only people in TV commercials were brave enough to say. Instead she changed the subject.

"Did you finish your career project?" she asked.

"Mine is twenty pages long," Ashley said. "My mother says that's longer than a lot of papers people write in *college*. It's on neurosurgery. My mother says that medicine is the most prestigious career, and surgery is the most prestigious kind of medicine, and neurosurgery is the most prestigious kind of surgery."

"Mine's on neurosurgery, too," Heather said miserably.

"How many pages?" Ashley demanded.

Heather didn't answer.

"Come on, I told first."

"Twelve. Well, eleven, really. . . ."

"Well, maybe since Mrs. McIntyre's so pregnant, she'll like short papers better," Cally said loyally. "She's too busy getting cribs and car seats ready to want to read a bunch of long, boring career reports."

"That's not true," Ashley said. "The work comes after you have the baby. All she has to do now is sit around and be fat."

It was time for Cally to change the subject again. She tried to think of a topic Ashley couldn't brag about. But maybe such a topic didn't exist.

The bell rang. Relieved, Cally carried her cafeteria tray to the conveyor belt. Her report on aerodynamics engineering had twenty-three pages. Three pages more than Ashley's! But she hadn't said anything, since she hadn't wanted to make Heather feel even worse. It was too bad Cally was such a nice person. It would have been fun to see Ashley's face.

Social studies came right after lunch. When the girls reached the classroom, Mrs. McIntyre wasn't there. Instead Miss Wellington, the principal, stood by the chalkboard, talking to a curly-haired man with a curly dark beard.

"Boys and girls," Miss Wellington said, when the children had taken their seats, "I have some exciting news. Mrs. McIntyre went to the hospital yesterday afternoon, and at four o'clock this morning Monica Elizabeth was born."

The class broke into cheers.

"We weren't expecting Monica for another month, so this has caught everyone by surprise. But we're very lucky to have found an outstanding teacher to take Mrs. McIntyre's place. Mr. Feinberg will be your teacher for the rest of the school year, and I hope you'll do your best to make him feel welcome."

The applause this time was more subdued. A new baby was exciting; a new teacher was a little bit scary.

Miss Wellington shook Mr. Feinberg's hand vigorously and then bustled away. The class looked at Mr. Feinberg. Mr. Feinberg looked at the class.

"I'm new," he said finally. "I'm new to teaching, and I'm new to this school. I don't know how Ms. McIntyre did things, but I'm probably going to be doing some things differently. Let's use today to get warmed up, okay? We'll pick up with the lesson plans on Monday."

With a bold hand he scrawled across the chalkboard: "Resolved: The American colonies should remain loyal to King George III."

"Have you ever had a debate?" he asked. "No? Well, you

are about to have one. I want half of you—those in the first two rows—to think up arguments in favor of the resolution I've written on the chalkboard. The rest of you think up arguments on the other side. All right? Half of you should be thinking of reasons why the Revolutionary War was a bad idea; the other half, reasons why it was a good idea."

Justin raised his hand. "We don't do the Revolutionary War in sixth grade."

"When do you 'do' it?" Mr. Feinberg asked.

"American history is fifth grade. And then we'll get it again when we get to high school—in ninth grade, I think."

"Then you've all 'done' the Revolution at least once, so I presume you understand the question. It may come as a surprise"—Mr. Feinberg consulted Mrs. McIntyre's seating chart—"Justin, but you may be called upon to discuss American history even in years when you're not officially 'doing' it in school. Okay, someone in Group One, why was the American Revolution a bad idea?"

No hands went up. Cally tried to remember everything she knew about the Revolutionary War, but fifth grade seemed a long time ago. The Boston Tea Party. Paul Revere. No taxation without representation. She had remembered a lot more on the day of the test, but she had forgotten most of it the day afterward. Besides, everyone knew that the American Revolution *wasn't* a bad idea.

"All right, we'll do the easier half first. Why was the Revolution a good idea?"

Ashley was in Group Two. She waved her hand right away. "No taxation without representation," she said.

"Meaning?"

A long pause. "If the British were going to, you know, tax us, then we should have representation and stuff."

"Is representation the same as independence?"

"Well, we couldn't get representation any other way. They wouldn't give it to us."

"And what exactly is the link between taxation and representation? Why should the two go together?"

Cally's palms were damp. Mr. Feinberg asked too many questions. But Ashley came through with another answer.

"It isn't fair. If you take somebody's money, they ought to get a say in how you spend it."

"Okay, good," Mr. Feinberg said. Maybe Ashley *was* gifted and talented, after all. "So, you people on the other side, give her an argument. Why was the Revolution a bad idea?"

Still no hands. Of course taxation without representation was unfair. What could anybody say against that?

Scott spoke up. "We might have lost."

"Excellent," Mr. Feinberg said. Cally felt a pang of jealousy. "Sure, successful revolutions seem like a good idea two centuries after they've succeeded. It's easy to forget that the vast majority of attempted revolutions fail. And on the eve of the American Revolution, there was no reason for anyone to think this one would be the exception.

"Any other reasons? Remember, the colonists were still subjects of the Crown. Wasn't it disloyal for them to rise up against their government? How would you feel today if, say, California or Pennsylvania rebelled against our government?"

"That's different," Justin said. "They don't have taxation without representation."

"Forget taxation without representation," Mr. Feinberg

said impatiently. "That's just a slogan. Don't mouth back something you memorized. Make your own points in your own words."

He looked at the seating chart again. "You, Heather, how would you feel if California declared its independence?"

Cally scrunched down in her seat, trying to make herself invisible so that Mr. Feinberg wouldn't call on her. The whole discussion was so unfair. No one had thought about the Revolutionary War in a whole year, and now they were expected to come up with opinions on it, at the drop of a hat, right out of their heads. Cally could have had a lot of opinions if he had made it a regular assignment and given them time to go to the library and look things up.

At last it was time for the bell.

"I almost forgot," Mr. Feinberg said. "You had some projects due today." Quickly he strode up and down the aisles collecting them. Cally felt better when she saw hers, twenty-three pages long, added to the top of the pile.

"My, you're a bunch of long-winded kids," Mr. Feinberg said, as the stack grew heavier. "Didn't anyone ever tell you that brevity is the soul of wit? Short and sweet, that's how I like them. Okay, class is dismissed. Oh, and class, you have good minds. Don't be afraid to use them."

Chapter 5

Cally made her own pigtails on Saturday morning, Margaret checking to be sure the part was straight. While she waited for Chuck to come, she practiced the piano, working her way through a Clementi sonatina. First she played with painstaking slowness, then gradually increased her speed. "Every note perfect every time," was how Mrs. Randolph taught her. You played as slowly as you needed to in order to stay note perfect, speeding up only when you had mastered a piece completely at the slow tempo.

By the time the doorbell rang, Cally's fingers were flying over the keys and she was lost in the pleasure of the music.

"Was that you playing?" Chuck asked, when Cally let him in. "It sounded just like a record."

Cally glowed at the praise. "Well, I've been taking lessons for five years."

"Can you play 'California, Here I Come'?"

"No, I just play classical music." That sounded stuck up, so Cally added, "I guess I could play it if I had the sheet music."

"You wouldn't need music for a tune like that." Chuck sat down on the piano bench and, after a couple of false starts, with one finger plunked out the opening notes of "California, Here I Come." He stumbled through it once and then played it again from beginning to end, throwing in a few chords with his left hand.

"You're good!" Cally said, surprised and a little bit miffed. "How many years have you taken lessons?"

"None. I can't read music or anything. I just mess around."

"Well, you sure sound like you've had lessons," Cally said crossly. "How did you know where to put all those chords?"

"I just put them where I thought they'd sound good. Come on, sing along. 'Ocean City, here we come. . . .' "

As she had the first time, Cally joined in. Their voices soared along with the melody, adding la-la-las where they couldn't think of words.

When they finished, Cally wasn't mad at Chuck anymore. It had been too much fun clowning around at the piano together. From the doorway, Margaret applauded. Steven, right behind her, clapped, too.

"Yay, Steven!" he said happily. He took for granted that all applause was meant for him. Cally hoped he wouldn't grow up to be another Ashley.

Chuck pulled her to a different neighborhood this time, where the houses were older and closer together. Cally felt the old fear creep back over her when she rang her first doorbell, but once she started in talking it gave way to a pleasant, tingly excitement. More people were home on a Saturday morning, as Chuck had predicted. Soon her list of subscribers had grown to fifteen names.

At the next house a man came to the door in his bathrobe, his face contorted with rage.

"What the hell do you think you're doing?" he bellowed.

Cally swallowed. Was she supposed to answer or not?

"Did it ever occur to you that some people like to sleep on a Saturday morning? That some people were up very late last night, and this is their one chance all week to sleep in? Did that ever enter your head?"

Apparently this time the man expected her to say something. "Did it?" he repeated.

"I—it's eleven-thirty," Cally whispered. At her house Steven got everyone up at seven. "I didn't think—"

"Well, next time," the man said with withering sarcasm, "next time, maybe you will."

He slammed the door. Cally began to hobble back down the path, willing herself not to cry. She had this terrible habit of crying whenever anyone was mean to her. She hadn't cried when she broke her foot, not once, even when the pain was sharpest. She would never have cried at the gymnastics meet, the way Ashley had. But let someone speak to her in a harsh tone of voice, and she couldn't hold back the tears.

"Cally! What's the matter?"

At the sympathy in Chuck's voice, Cally broke down. "He said—he said—" She was crying so hard she couldn't get the words out. "He said I—woke—him—up."

"Oh, he did, did he?" Chuck grabbed Cally's arm. "Come on, we're going back there."

Before she could protest, Chuck had dragged her back to the man's door. He banged on it furiously with the brass knocker.

The same man came to the door again. "Dammit," he shouted, but Chuck cut him off.

"Listen, mister, maybe we woke you up, and if we did we apologize. But if that's the biggest problem you have in your life, then I've got to say that I'm not going to sit up nights feeling sorry for you. Look at this girl—look at her." He pointed at Cally. "Her foot's broken so bad the doctors don't know if she'll ever walk without crutches again. But, no, you're the only one who has problems.

"And listen"—the man tried to interrupt but Chuck kept on talking—"why do you think she's out selling these lousy papers, anyway? Did you ever wonder about that? It's because she needs the money. She needs it bad. Her father's out of work at the mill, and they don't know if they can pay the doctor who's trying to fix her foot. But, no, mister, you're the only one who has problems."

"I don't have to listen to this," the man said, but he seemed a bit shaken.

"No, you don't," Chuck said. "You can slam the door in our faces and go back to your nap. Heck, there are kids starving all over the world. What's it to you? Especially if it gets in the way of your sleep. But let me say one more thing, and it's the last thing I'm going to say. If I turned away a little girl on crutches because I was too cheap to buy one stinking newspaper from her, then *I* wouldn't be able to sleep. No, sir, my conscience wouldn't let me."

"What's going on, George?" A gentle-faced woman joined the mean man at the door.

"Kids selling a newspaper," the mean man said. "Woke me up, too," he said, but this time under his breath.

"Well, let's buy one. How much is it?"

"Seven dollars and twenty cents," Chuck said. "Delivered to your door in all weather."

Cally didn't know what to say as Chuck settled her in the

wagon for the ride home. Everything he had said to the mean man was a lie. Her broken foot would be healed in six weeks; her father wasn't out of work at the mill; her father didn't even work at a mill.

"I thought a good salesman doesn't lie," she said finally.

"I didn't do that as a salesman." Chuck turned around and looked at Cally. "He should have known better than to make you cry. Nobody picks on my friends, not if I have anything to say about it."

"They bought one, though," Cally pointed out.

Chuck grinned. "Hey, if they really wanted to, I wasn't going to stop them."

Cally grinned back, even though she felt she shouldn't encourage him. She couldn't help being grateful that Chuck had come to her defense; he had done a better job sticking up for her against the mean man than she had done sticking up for Heather against Ashley. But why couldn't he have done it without telling so many whoppers? Chuck never stopped to think before he plunged ahead; Cally was always afraid to take the plunge. It would be nice if they were both somewhere in the middle.

When they reached Cally's block, Chuck asked, "When do you have to be home? Can you come to my house for lunch?"

"Sure. I don't have to be home at any special time." Without her usual Saturday-afternoon gymnastics workout, empty hours stretched luxuriously ahead of her.

No one was home at Cally's, so she left a note on the refrigerator: WENT TO CHUCK'S FOR LUNCH. BE BACK LATER.

"They probably won't even notice I'm gone. Saturdays are kind of hectic at my house."

"Just you wait. You haven't seen hectic till you've met the Fosters," Chuck said proudly.

Cally wasn't exaggerating when she said that Saturdays were busy in the Lippincott family. Cally's mother taught an adult education course on investment finance called "The Economy and You." Her father ran ten miles with his running group, which was also his great books group. Every week the members read a great book of the Western world, and they discussed it together as they ran. Or maybe *read* wasn't the right word. They *absorbed* a great book. Mr. Lippincott listened to cassette tapes of great books in the car as he commuted back and forth to work. Even Steven had a full schedule. Margaret took him to a toddlers' swimming class at the Y and then to storytelling at the public library.

Usually Cally had a special Saturday morning activity, too. The university ran various six-week workshops for gifted students, but "A First Look at Relativity" had finished a week ago, and "A First Look at the Russian Revolution" wouldn't begin until sometime in April. You didn't actually have to be gifted to go to the workshops. You just had to have parents who were willing to spend a hundred dollars for each of the programs.

Sometimes it made Cally tired to think about everything the Lippincott family did on the weekends. And during the week, too. But Cally's parents had read books on time management, and they had learned how to make every minute count.

"How far is it to your house?" Cally asked, once she had settled herself again in the wagon.

"It's pretty close. It's over by Kennedy Middle School. But

that should be your school, too. How come you don't go there?"

"I go to Forest Glen Day School," Cally said. "It's private."

"La-dee-dah," Chuck said cheerfully. "I could tell from your house that your parents are rich."

"No, they're not," Cally protested. "They're just—"

"Rich," Chuck said. "That's okay. I like rich people. I plan to be one myself someday. And rich people can afford a lot of newspapers. Speaking of which, have your parents subscribed yet? I got your sister, but I'd think your parents would want one, too."

"Margaret's not my sister," Cally explained. "She lives with us to take care of Steven."

"La-dee-dah," Chuck said again. "Anyway, she's nice. She seems to like you a lot."

"I like her, too," Cally said. She would hate it next year when Margaret graduated and moved away.

When they reached Chuck's house, Cally saw why Chuck had thought her parents were rich. The Fosters' house was a one-story shoebox, hardly bigger, from the front, than the Lippincotts' oversized two-car garage. It could have used a fresh coat of yellow paint. Behind a sagging chain-link fence, the yard was trampled to bare dirt in places and covered with tricycles, garden hoses, rusted rakes, roller skates.

But it had a welcoming look. A spanking new American flag flew from a makeshift flagpole, and pansies overflowed from window boxes. Three small girls with dirty, smiling faces waited on the front steps, each wearing a pirate hat folded from newspaper. The newspaper, Cally assumed, was the *County Times*.

"Hi, Chuck!" They ran up to him for kisses. "What's your girlfriend's name?" the tallest girl demanded.

Cally waited for Chuck to tell them angrily that she wasn't his girlfriend, just a friend who helped him sell newspapers.

"Cally," Chuck told them.

"What happened to her foot?"

"Why don't you ask her?"

"What happened to your foot?"

"I broke it," Cally said.

Chuck helped Cally into the house, the little girls bringing up the rear of the parade. The living room was bursting with chairs, tables, toys, knickknacks—many broken, and all in need of a good dusting. Chuck's family probably didn't have a cleaning lady come in two days a week the way Cally's did.

They found Mrs. Foster in the kitchen. She looked nice, with Chuck's wide smile and dancing blue eyes. Spread out before her on the kitchen table were dozens of parts of some household appliance.

"The iron," she announced. "Taking it apart is a lot easier than putting it back together."

"Mom, this is Cally. She's come for lunch."

"But if it's too much trouble—" Cally began, wondering where on earth they would eat. She hadn't yet seen an uncluttered surface.

"It's no trouble at all," Mrs. Foster said, "if you don't mind using your lap as a table. That's the nice thing about chaos. Nothing makes it any worse. Here, Cally, have a seat and see if you can figure out how to make a steam iron out of all this."

Cally sat down. She hoped Mrs. Foster was joking about the iron. No one in Cally's family was the least bit handy. Her parents had once called the furnace repairman only to find they could have gotten the furnace to work themselves simply by turning it on.

Fascinated, Cally watched as Chuck and his mother broiled hot dogs, toasted buns, opened a bag of potato chips, and poured plastic cups of Kool-Aid. The tallest little girl—Anna—made newspaper hats for Chuck and Cally. The middle-sized little girl—Susie—played beauty parlor on Cally's hair. Mary, the smallest one, made Cally read aloud to her from *The Little Engine That Could.*

Cally had forgotten how much she liked the story of the brave little engine who made it over the mountain just by believing he could do it. It reminded her of Chuck, who had told her the day they met, "You have to believe in yourself, right?" The contest ended next Saturday, only a week away. *I HOPE we win, I HOPE we win, I HOPE we win,* she said to herself.

Chapter 6

Six More Days

On Sunday Chuck and Cally tried something different. Instead of going from door to door, they headed to Westmark Mall. It was Chuck's idea, naturally. "That place is swarming with people who want to buy things, right? Well, for pennies a day they can buy the *County Times*."

Mr. Lippincott had agreed to drive them to the mall when it opened at one, and Chuck bicycled over to the house at a quarter of. Cally had hoped they could leave right away, but her mother insisted on meeting her new friend. Right away Cally could tell her parents didn't like the new friend as much as they liked the old ones.

"What's your favorite subject in school?" Mrs. Lippincott asked Chuck, as she passed around glasses of lemonade and a plate of Danish butter cookies. It sounded as if she were interviewing him.

"I like them all pretty well."

"But there must be one you like best," Mrs. Lippincott persisted.

"Gym, I guess."

One wrong answer.

"Do you have any hobbies?" Mr. Lippincott asked next. "I

imagine a boy your age is nuts about science. When I was a kid it was astronomy. I built my own telescope and spent half my time thinking I'd be the one to find a tenth planet. How about you?"

"I like to sell things."

Another wrong answer.

"Speaking of which," Chuck said, "I'm sure you'll want to subscribe to the *County Times* now that Cally's in the business."

Mrs. Lippincott didn't look as if she were sure of that at all, but Mr. Lippincott reached for his wallet.

"That makes one hundred forty-three," Chuck said. "If any of your friends or relatives want one, just let me know."

The mall was crowded. Cally was more used to her crutches now (Margaret was right about some things), and they were glad they had decided not to bring the wagon. It would have been awkward pulling it through the throngs of shoppers. To Cally's relief, Chuck suggested that they work together. Selling papers in the mall was even scarier than going from door to door. It was so public. If a mean man yelled at her, fifty strangers would hear.

They began by going up to people resting on the benches. Most were senior citizens, so business was slow.

"When people are retired, they watch their money," Chuck said. "Old people know how fast pennies a day can turn into dollars a week."

They discovered that if the first person they approached agreed to buy a paper, others within hearing often bought one, too. If the first person in any cluster of benches said, "No, thank you," four or five other no-thank-you's would follow in a row. After a few tries, they learned to target potential customers carefully. Teenagers were the worst; younger couples without children were the best. In an hour they had sold eleven more subscriptions. One hundred fifty-four.

"I'll buy you an ice cream cone," Chuck said. "Any flavor your heart desires."

"Strawberry," Cally said. She had never had a boy buy her anything before. It made her feel shy and self-conscious, as if the trip to the shopping mall were a real, true date.

As Cally waited on a bench for Chuck to bring back the cones, Ashley and her mother, burdened with shopping bags, emerged from the mall's most expensive store. Cally hoped Ashley wouldn't see her and come over to say hello. Chuck would be back any minute. She wouldn't mind if Ashley noticed she was practically on a date with a boy, but she'd be embarrassed if Chuck tried to sell them the *County Times*. He didn't have to sell one to *everybody*. And after two minutes of Ashley, Chuck would think Cally went to a school full of snobs.

"Hi, Cally!"

It was too late. Ashley was upon her.

"You shouldn't wear your hair in pigtails. It makes you look about eight years old. Mom, show her the new dress you bought me. Guess what it cost, Cally." She lowered her voice. "It cost a *lot*."

Before Cally could say anything, Chuck arrived, a dripping double-decker cone in each hand.

Sighing, Cally made the introductions. Caught off-guard, Ashley's face gave away how impressed she was that Cally knew a cute boy who would bring her an ice cream cone.

"Oh, Cally, did you hear?" Ashley was herself again. "Heather applied to Camp Danforth, too, and she didn't get in. Her mother told my mother at their aerobics class. I think I'm the only one in the whole school who's going. They only take one out of five, you know. It's more selective than the Ivy League!"

"I know," Cally said. "You told me."

"But the terrible thing is, I have a rich aunt, I mean really rich, and it turns out that she was planning to take me to Paris this summer if I didn't get in to Danforth. Paris, France! But nobody in their right mind would turn down Danforth."

"Of course you're going to Danforth," Ashley's mother said. "There'll be plenty of other summers to go to Europe."

"Hey," Chuck said abruptly. "Do you want to buy a subscription to the *County Times*? Cally and I are selling them. Just pennies a day. Delivered to your door in all weather."

"I really don't think . . . " Ashley's mother looked uncomfortable. "And I'm sure you children aren't supposed to be soliciting here in the mall. Don't let a policeman overhear you bothering people."

"We don't bother people," Chuck said staunchly. "We give them an opportunity to subscribe to their own local paper. It's practically a public service. So what do you say?"

"I'm sorry, dear," Ashley's mother said, not sounding sorry at all, "but I don't think so."

"Well, I guess if you can't afford it. . . ."

Cally could see Ashley's mother bristle at the idea that she wasn't buying the *County Times* because she was too cheap to shell out seven dollars and twenty cents.

"Oh, all right." She looked around to make sure no one had overheard Chuck's remark. "I'll take it. On a trial basis."

When Ashley and her mother had gone, Chuck asked, "Are all the girls in your school like that?"

"I go to my school, and I'm not like that."

"No," Chuck said. He reached over and gently straightened one of Cally's pigtails. "No, you're not."

One hundred fifty-five.

Five More Days

According to the terms of Mr. Lippincott's compromise, Monday was a science and math day. Cally's mother had bought her a special sixth-grade math workbook, full of extra problems to practice on. The math problems in the workbook were twice as hard as the ones in the regular textbook, and three times as boring. Cally would be twenty by the time she had finished all of them.

"Do as many as you can this afternoon," her mother told her on the way home from school. "I'll check them for you before dinner."

Monday was also the day that Margaret had afternoon classes at the university and Cally's mother worked at home. Cally loved her mother, but life was undeniably easier when Margaret was in charge. With Margaret, Cally could pretend to study, propping a book up in front of her as she daydreamed. Not with Mrs. Lippincott.

Even Steven had to work on Mondays. That day they drilled his great composers flashcards. The box of flashcards came with a cassette recording of passages from famous musical works. When it played the opening bars of the *Eroica* Symphony, Mrs. Lippincott would hold up a flashcard of Beethoven's scowling face. And Steven would say Beethoven's name, or something that sounded like it if you listened very hard. In all there were fifty passages for him to identify. "Make your child a prodigy," it said on the flashcards box.

At five-thirty, the phone rang. Cally quickly snatched it up, glad of any interruption from the workbook.

"Hi, Cally, it's Chuck! One hundred seventy-two!"

Four More Days

It rained on Tuesday. "You don't have to come if you don't want," Chuck told Cally.

"I do want."

So they set off together, Cally riding in the wagon, since every day they had to go farther to find a neighborhood where they hadn't been before. From beneath the hood of her yellow rubber rain slicker, Cally peered out at a world of sodden lawns and dripping hedges. The rain fell steadily.

As she rang the doorbell of her first house, Cally felt exactly like the pathetic child Chuck had made her out to be in the story to the mean man. She stood soaked, shivering, looking in through the curtains at someone else's warm, cheery home. In a fairy tale, the door would swing open and there would stand Cally's fairy godmother, ready with a touch of her magic wand to transport the miserable waif to an enchanted kingdom. But in real life, when the door swung open, there stood Mr. Feinberg.

Somehow Cally stumbled through her *County Times* speech, praying he wouldn't recognize her. After all, he had her class only one period a day, and so far she hadn't said a syllable.

But he did. "You're Cally Lippincott, aren't you? From sixth period."

Cally nodded. She steeled herself for a question on the American Revolution.

"I didn't know you could talk," he said. "Sure, I'll take a paper. I like to see the spirit of enterprise in kids today."

He ushered her into his foyer, not seeming to mind her dripping all over his pretty, patterned rug.

"So we have an entrepreneur in our midst," he said thoughtfully, counting out his money. "Somehow I wouldn't have picked you for that role. You sit in class as if you're afraid I'm going to bite your head off. But the way I see it is, if you can knock on a stranger's door and talk him into buying a newspaper, you can put up your hand in class and talk the rest of us into agreeing with one of your opinions. Of course, you have to have an opinion first. You do have opinions, don't you?"

Cally didn't say anything.

Mr. Feinberg sighed. "Well, good luck with sales."

Opinions! Cally thought as she retreated down the teacher's front walk. She had plenty of opinions, and one of them was: *Mr. Feinberg is impossible.*

By the end of the afternoon, the total stood at one hundred ninety-two.

Three More Days

Mr. Feinberg called on Cally in class on Wednesday. They had begun a new unit on economics, but so far Cally's mother's possible future Nobel Prize wasn't helping Cally one bit.

They had been assigned to read a chapter on the difference between the American economy and the Soviet economy. The American economy is a market economy, based on the law of supply and demand. The Soviet economy is a planned economy, with prices set by the government.

"Okay, gang," Mr. Feinberg started in. "What are some reasons for having a market economy? Cally?"

Cally's heart sank. The textbook had given a couple of reasons: A market economy is more efficient, and a market economy leaves more room for freedom. But if she gave the answer about efficiency, he might ask her why efficiency was a good thing. If she gave the answer about freedom, he might ask why freedom was a good thing. And then what would she say?

"Because—" Cally stopped. Efficiency was good because it made prices lower. And freedom was good because—well, just because it was.

"Because?" Mr. Feinberg repeated, smiling at Cally to encourage her. "A couple of reasons should come easily to mind."

Cally felt her cheeks flush as red as her hair. She knew whatever she said wouldn't be what Mr. Feinberg wanted to hear. She stared down at her desk, refusing to be encouraged, until at last the teacher gave up and called on someone else.

"Justin?"

"A market system is more efficient."

"What's so great about efficiency?"

"Well, it means prices are lower, so people don't have to spend so much on cars or groceries and they can spend more on things they really want."

"Good," Mr. Feinberg said, and Cally thought, *I could have said that.* But how could she have known in advance that it was the answer Mr. Feinberg wanted?

When Chuck telephoned Cally that evening, the total had risen to two hundred and five.

"But we don't know how many subscriptions other kids sold," Cally complained. "For all we know, someone else sold three hundred and five. Or four hundred and five."

"True," Chuck said. "That's why we can't rest for a minute, however many we get. But I do know two things. One is that Jim McTaggart—he's another real go-getter in my school—well, he's sold a hundred sixty-seven. He was bragging to me about it this morning. I acted crushed, of course. And, two, last year's winning total was one hundred and ninety."

"Which we've beaten already," Cally said. "By fifteen."

"And by the end of the week," Chuck said, "we'll beat it by fifty."

Two More Days

On Thursday Cally worked as hard as she had ever worked in her life. She hurried from house to house on her crutches, leaned on doorbells, turned on all her charm, tried not to take no for an answer. But she was still no match for Chuck. Chuck talked so fast, with so much energy and confidence, that people were knocked down, run over, squashed flat, before they knew what had hit them.

Cally was late for dinner that night, but she didn't care whether she got a scolding. Two hundred and twenty-seven! Nobody could beat them now—nobody.

One More Day

Cally knew better than to try to get out of her piano lesson, but every minute at her lesson was a minute she could have been selling newspapers. She poured all her frustrated energy into her playing, to Mrs. Randolph's delight. And before Cally left, for pennies a day and delivery in all weather, Mrs. Randolph, too, was a new subscriber to the *County Times*.

The contest ended on Saturday at noon. Chuck and Cally kept on selling up until the moment they had to leave for the *County Times* office in Rockville. When they had to stop, the total stood at two hundred forty-two.

"The thing that kills me," Chuck said, "is that if we had gone to just one more house it might have been two hundred forty-three."

Mr. Foster drove them there. He was a big, burly, silent man, with hands like hams and gentle eyes.

"Now, you kids won't be disappointed if you lose, will you?" he asked, as he pulled his pickup truck into the *Times* parking lot.

"Sure, we'll be disappointed," Chuck said. "But we'll live. Besides," he whispered to Cally, "we aren't going to lose."

They were third in line at the cashier's window to turn in their money and the list of names.

When their turn came, the cashier took one look at their total and squealed. "Don, come here a minute!" she called to the manager. "This kid sold two hundred and forty-two!"

"I think we have our first-prize winner," Don said, smiling broadly at Chuck and Cally. "Now, nothing's official, mind you, till we've gone over all the entries and double-checked everything. But so far, I can say, no one's touched this. And the contest closes in—let's see—three minutes."

Chuck squeezed Cally's hand. Her heart was bursting with happiness.

Another kid came in, a girl, older than they were. They heard her log in at one hundred twenty-two.

Two minutes left. One. Cally felt as if it were New Year's Eve, and they were waiting for the famous ball to slide down the building in Times Square, New York City, with the whole world watching and the announcer chanting the countdown as animated champagne glasses danced on the TV screen.

The door swung open one last time. A fat boy, dressed in a polka-dot clown costume, panted up to the cashier's window.

"Here," he gasped. "I got one more in the parking lot, so I haven't added their money in yet."

He hung on to the counter, breathing heavily.

"And the total is?" the cashier asked.

Cally stopped breathing. Chuck held her hand tightly.

"Two hundred and fifty."

Chapter 7

From years of gymnastics meets, Cally had learned how to lose. First, act like you don't care. Next, get away from the scene of defeat fast. And, finally, *don't* care. Anything you couldn't win at wasn't worth caring about. After a gymnastics meet, Cally would pump the first-place winner's hand, act thrilled about her own third-place ribbon, vanish abruptly into the locker room, and remind herself that she had never liked gymnastics, anyway.

Now she smiled automatically, the kind of smile that stayed fixed on your face even when you were struggling not to cry. To have come so close, after all that work! Even the second-place prize of fifty dollars was no consolation. Tears crowded up behind her eyelids, despite her, and she turned to flee to the parking lot.

Chuck held her hand fast.

"Wait," he said. He sounded angry. At her? At the boy in the clown suit? "I have to find out how he did it."

"It's too late," Cally said, twisting her hand free.

"It's not too late to learn something from it," Chuck said. "This guy did something right that I did wrong, and I want to know what it was."

So that was it: Chuck was mad at himself. They waited as

the clown boy finished tallying his money and signing the contest affadavit. Then Chuck pounced.

"Congratulations!" he said, all trace of anger gone from his voice. He clapped the clown on the back, and the plump boy blushed with pleasure.

"Congratulations," Cally echoed.

"Do you mind if I ask how you did it?" Chuck asked. "Because me and my partner here came in right behind you. We had two hundred and forty-two."

"Whew, that was close," the clown said. "I don't know. I never missed a day ringing doorbells. I must have rung a million, at least. And the clown suit helped a lot. People don't know what to expect when they see a clown on their doorstep, so I kind of caught them off-guard. I made up a flier, too. Here, I have an extra one." He pulled it from his sheaf of papers and handed it to Chuck and Cally.

EXTRA, EXTRA, READ ALL ABOUT IT! the flier said. AN INTRODUCTORY OFFER YOU CAN'T PASS UP FOR THE COUNTY TIMES! Underneath the headline was a picture of a clown holding a bunch of balloons. Inside each balloon was written one good thing about the *County Times*: MOST CLASSIFIED ADS! HIGH SCHOOL SPORTS SCORES! PENNIES A DAY! DELIVERED IN ALL WEATHER!

"Can I keep this?" Chuck asked. The boy nodded. Chuck smoothed out a crumpled corner on the flier and folded it into a neat square, which he tucked reverently into his shirt pocket. "Chuck Foster," he said, and offered the clown his hand.

"Danny DeMotto."

They shook hands, and the clown went on his way.

"He deserved to win," Chuck said to Cally. "That's the part that hurts the most. He beat us fair and square."

When Cally lost at gymnastics or didn't get a leading role in ballet, the worst of it was breaking the news to her parents. But Chuck just flashed a thumbs-down sign to his father as he helped Cally hoist herself, crutches and all, into the truck.

"How much did you lose by?" Mr. Foster asked.

Chuck held his thumb and forefinger half an inch apart. "Man, oh man," he said, "we lost to the best."

Cally tried to keep the quaver out of her voice. "Your trip— to Ocean City."

For a moment Chuck looked downcast. Then he grinned. "As my grandma used to say, there's more ways to kill a cat than drowning it in butter. There're probably tons of contests that send you to Ocean City if you win. You know, Why I Like Ocean City in twenty-five words or less. Or I could get a job and earn the money. Pop, how much money would I need to take all of us, and Cally, to Ocean City for a week?"

Cally waited for Mr. Foster to say, "Don't worry, son. If you want to go, we're going!" The Fosters had to go someplace on vacation, right? Why not Ocean City, if that was where Chuck had his heart set on going? Last summer Cally's family had gone to Nova Scotia, and the year before to Hawaii, taking Margaret with them, as well.

"If you can earn two hundred dollars, I'll find a way to come up with the rest," Mr. Foster said. "How's that for a deal? Even then, it's going to be tight. Your mother and I decided a long time ago that we'd get all of you kids an education if we did nothing else, and I'm not robbing your college fund for frills."

"What kind of a job can you get if you're only eleven?" Cally asked, indignant on Chuck's behalf.

Chuck ticked them off on his fingers. "Shoveling snow, raking leaves, mowing lawns." Spring was hardly the time of year for any of those. "A paper route—but I'm pretty tired of newspapers now, aren't you? Walking rich people's dogs for them. Recycling cans and bottles. I don't know. You think of something."

Cally thought. The six-week unit on careers hadn't spent a single day on real jobs kids could do right now. Certainly aerodynamics engineering and neurosurgery were out of the question. What jobs were open to children? They could be Peter and Wendy in a movie version of *Peter Pan*. They could model kids' clothes in a department-store catalog. They could join the circus and help the lion tamer or perform on the flying trapeze.

"I can't think of any ideas that aren't stupid," she confessed.

"Let's hear one! The stupider the better."

He had asked for it. "Join the circus and fly on the flying trapeze."

Chuck looked thoughtful. "You're good at gymnastics. Of course, there's your cast—"

"*And* I hate heights."

Chuck seemed not to hear. "Circuses," he said, almost to himself.

"Besides, there're no circuses around here, anyway."

"I have it!" Chuck yelled, so loudly that his father slowed the truck. "Think, Cally. What was Danny DeMotto's big secret?"

"The flier and— You mean, we should be clowns?" She was about to explain that she hated clowns as much as she hated heights, but Chuck kept on talking.

"Rent-a-Clown," he said triumphantly. "Clowns for all occasions. Birthday parties. Bar mitzvahs. Weddings. Funerals."

"Funerals?"

"When a car dealership opens. At county fairs. Visiting the sick in hospitals. Delivering balloons, ten dollars a bunch. Office parties. Advertising—you know, handing out circulars on the corner outside the store. Old folks' homes. Parades. Baseball games."

"But not *funerals*," Cally protested.

"Pop?" Chuck asked. "Can you take us to the public library?"

Mr. Foster shook his head in good-natured disbelief. "Whatever you say, son."

"Because Cally and I need to get some books on how to be clowns. We need them right away."

"I'm sorry I'm late," Cally called to her parents, after Chuck's father had deposited her back home with half the library books. "We stopped at the library." She couldn't have had an excuse they would have liked better, and it was even true.

"Who won the contest?" her mother asked, coming into the living room.

In the excitement of the new venture, Cally had almost forgotten the pain of defeat. "A boy named Danny DeMotto. But we came in second."

"Are those for a project at school?" Mrs. Lippincott eyed the library books. "I didn't know you had something due."

"Not really," Cally said. Few school projects required students to read *Clowning for Fun and Profit, Magic Tricks Galore,* and *101 Knock-Knock Jokes.*

Steven ran in before Mrs. Lippincott could examine the titles more closely. He was singing "Old MacDonald Had a Farm" at the top of his lungs. He had been singing it when Cally left for the *County Times* office that morning, and she suspected he had been singing it ever since. No one could fault Steven on diligence in practicing.

"How about singing another song for a while?" his mother asked.

"No!"

"How about singing 'Frère Jacques'?"

"No!"

"Or 'Du, Du Liegst Mir im Herzen'?" It was a point of pride for the Lippincotts that Steven could sing in three languages.

"No!"

"Old MacDonald" continued even louder.

"I guess this is what they call the terrible twos," Mrs. Lippincott said to Cally, "and he isn't even two yet. Which reminds me. His birthday is a week from today, and I suppose we really should have some kind of party. Nothing too elaborate, just the five other children from his toddlers' swimming class and their parents. I'm counting on you to be a big help, Cally. How I'll entertain six two-year-olds for two hours, I don't know. It's hard enough to entertain one for five minutes."

A light bulb flashed on in Cally's brain. Maybe this was the time to break the news to her mother about Rent-a-Clown.

"What about a clown?" she asked. "Or two clowns."

Her mother actually looked interested. "Where would I find a clown? I don't imagine I can look up Clowns in the yellow pages."

"Well, Chuck and I—now that the contest is over—we're going to start a business called Rent-a-Clown. We'll perform at kids' birthday parties and, you know, anywhere anybody needs a clown."

Cally could tell right away that her mother didn't like Rent-a-Clown any better than she had liked the door-to-door newspaper sales.

"I thought we had an agreement," Mrs. Lippincott said. "Your father and I agreed to let you help Chuck with his contest, and that's all we agreed to. If the contest is over, then it's back to your studies."

"But, Mom, I'm still studying as much as I ever did. Rent-a-Clown isn't instead of studying, it's instead of ballet and gymnastics, and I can't do those because of my broken foot. Remember?"

"But a broken foot doesn't stop you from clowning around, does it?" Mrs. Lippincott made it sound as if Cally had broken her foot on purpose, to get out of doing anything she didn't feel like doing. "I think you see far too much of Chuck as it is, Cally."

"Can't we just do Steven's party?" Cally pleaded. It might be better to coax her mother along one step at a time. "You thought the clowns were a good idea, until you knew it was us."

Mrs. Lippincott looked torn.

"You need something for those *six* two-year-olds. . . ."

"Oh, all right. But once your cast comes off, it'll be back to our regular routine."

I never want my cast to come off, then. I hate the regular routine, Cally almost said. She hadn't hated it before, but before she hadn't had Chuck for a friend and the prospect of launching their own business together. But she wasn't about to argue after her mother had given in.

"It's twenty dollars for an hour of clowning," Cally said. She and Chuck had worked out the price scale on the way home. Cally thought the fee was astronomical, but Chuck said you had to charge a lot or no one would take you seriously.

Sure enough, her mother didn't flinch. "I hope you two know what you're getting into," was all she said.

Cally had a twinge of doubt. When Chuck announced his Rent-a-Clown brainstorm, she had meant to tell him that she hated clowns, but the tidal wave of his enthusiasm had engulfed her as it had with the *County Times* sales contest. As far back as Cally could remember she had hated clowns. When she was three, a horrible, grinning clown had come up to her one day in a supermarket parking lot, and for days after she hadn't wanted to go outside for fear that more clowns would be lurking there. But how could she tell Chuck her clown-hating story when he was all fired up about a business called Rent-a-Clown? It would be like telling her father that she didn't want to do her career report on aerodynamics engineering. Cally hated to disappoint other people. She hated it more than anything.

Besides, maybe other children liked clowns. After all, Danny DeMotto had won the *County Times* contest wearing a clown suit. Cally certainly hoped other children liked clowns. In any case, she hadn't said anything when Chuck launched the idea, and it was too late to say anything now.

Chuck's mother made their costumes: billowing polka-dot clown suits that gathered into red ruffles at the wrists and ankles. Cally's was made to fit over her bulky cast. Margaret borrowed some greasepaint from an actor friend at the university and taught Cally how to put on a chalky white face with a gigantic red mouth and shiny red nose. One of the library books told how to make fright wigs out of coarse orange yarn.

On Monday, while Cally trudged through twenty more problems in the special math workbook, Chuck took a bus downtown to Merlin's House of Magic, a store crammed full of props for jokes and magic tricks. He spent half of the *County Times* prize money and came home with two bulging shopping bags to share with Cally on Tuesday. They emptied them out on Cally's family room floor.

"What's this?" she asked, pointing to a large plastic daisy.

"You bend down to smell it, and it squirts you, see?"

Cally squealed as the spray drenched her.

"That's good," Chuck said. "You have a very effective squeal. Can you do it even when you're not surprised?"

He squirted her again, and she gave another little scream.

"Perfect," Chuck said. "That goes in the act."

They tried out collapsible top hats, soft rubber bats to hit each other over the head with, trick pockets from which they could pull long strings of plastic salamis. Gradually the gags formed themselves into routines, interspersed with outrageously dumb jokes mined from the library humor collections. Chuck: "Last night I dreamed I ate a ten-pound marshmallow." Cally: "So?" Chuck: "So when I woke up my pillow was gone!" At the end of each joke Cally honked a rubber horn.

They practiced for hours, and Cally had so much fun that she found herself thinking, maybe clowns weren't so bad. Maybe Rent-a-Clown would be a big success, after all, and they would earn enough money to go to Ocean City. Maybe this time the Little Engine That Could would chug over the mountain.

Chapter 8

On Wednesday, Mr. Feinberg had the career reports. As soon as he laid the thick stack of papers in front of him on his desk, Cally's heart began to beat faster. She hoped he would give them back right away, instead of waiting until the end of the period, as some teachers did. She had done so poorly in class discussion so far that she wanted to see her A (or A + ?) as proof that Mr. Feinberg thought she was smart, after all.

Cally may be shy, she imagined the teacher saying, *but a girl with a twenty-three-page report on aerodynamics engineering is obviously no dummy.*

Her report had a yellow cover, and Cally strained to glimpse it in the pile. She thought she saw something yellow near the top, which was a good sign if Mr. Feinberg had arranged them in order from best to worst, but a bad sign if he had arranged them in order from worst to best. Honestly, though, how could she get less than an A? Her father's photographs alone were worth an A.

Mr. Feinberg looked out at the class for a long moment before he spoke. "When I give these back," he said finally, "you can save yourselves the trouble of looking for a grade. There isn't any. I gave occasional comments, but no grades."

He let the whispers and rustles die down before he continued.

"I give grades for your own work," he said, "not for the work of your parents."

In the stunned silence that followed only Ashley raised her hand. "My report *is* my own work," she said. "I worked very hard on it, too, and I think I should get an A."

Mr. Feinberg sifted through the pile and pulled out Ashley's fat report on neurosurgery.

"Very neatly typed," he said. "By you, I presume?"

"My mother typed it, but I don't see—"

"Fine," Mr. Feinberg said. "That much parental help I can accept. Did she type it just as you wrote it, or did she 'edit' it as she typed? Did she 'fix up' spelling, punctuation, grammar? Clarify and tighten sentences? Amplify some points?"

"Maybe a little bit."

"And maybe a lot. I'm sorry, Ashley, but this does not sound to me like a sentence a sixth-grader, even, shall we say, a highly gifted sixth-grader, would write: 'The nineteenth century saw the foundation of modern surgery, with the introduction of anesthetics, the discovery of antisepsis, and a greater knowledge of anatomy and physiology.' Do you even know what those words mean?"

"Most of them," Ashley insisted stubbornly.

"The report is illustrated with a number of color photographs, taken by . . .?"

"My father, but—"

"And diagrams of the central nervous system, drawn by . . .?"

"My father, but—"

"I can't give this a grade. Maybe Ms. McIntyre could, but I can't."

Instead of handing back the reports, Mr. Feinberg passed out blank sheets of yellow lined paper.

"For the rest of the period, you will write a brief essay entitled 'A Day in the Life of a . . . .' " He paused, looking at Ashley. "A neurosurgeon. Or a database manager. Whatever the subject of your career report. What they do all day, how they do it. *That* I can grade. Okay, gang, you have about thirty minutes. I'll give back your reports when you're done."

Cally wrote the title across the top of her paper: "A Day in the Life of an Aerodynamics Engineer." Her cheeks burned. She tried to remember everything she could about aerodynamics engineering, but only a few stray phrases came to mind. Something about lift and drag. About air being a viscous fluid. Wind tunnels. What did aerodynamics engineers do all day, besides die of boredom at the thought of themselves? What was it like to be one?

She wanted to leave the rest of the paper blank, to crumple it into a ball and throw it away, but she couldn't. She had to write something, anything. With a heavy heart she picked up her pencil and began: "An aerodynamics engineer studies lift and drag. He works in a wind tunnel. In the wind tunnel he learns many interesting facts about air, which is a viscous fluid."

"What's wrong?" Chuck asked after school on Thursday, as they prepared to practice their clowning routine for the last time before Steven's party.

"Nothing."

"You've been crying."

"No, I haven't."

"Okay, *don't* tell me, then," Chuck said, obviously hurt.

"It's just that I—well, I got a—bad grade."

"A B?" Chuck teased.

Cally had almost convinced herself that it would be a B. Until Mr. Feinberg had handed back the "Day in the Life" essays that afternoon, B had been the lowest grade she could imagine. She shook her head.

"A C?"

She shook her head again, willing herself not to cry in front of Chuck, but one tear spilled over.

"A D," she whispered.

Chuck gave a low whistle. "How did that happen?"

Cally told him how everything had gone wrong in social studies from the day Mr. Feinberg arrived.

"But you don't want to be an aerodynamics engineer, do you?"

Cally shuddered at the thought.

"Then why'd you pick aerodynamics engineering for your career report?"

My parents made me, Cally wanted to say. But that wasn't really true. It wasn't as if she had made any suggestions of her own and had had them overruled.

"My parents thought it up. They thought I'd be guaranteed to get an A if I wrote on something hard like that. They wanted me to get an A so much they practically did the whole report for me."

"You mean, like cheating?"

"No, like *helping*. Everyone's parents do it."

"Mine sure don't," Chuck said. "What's the fun of having someone else do your report for you? It might as well be anybody's, then. It's not really yours."

That was certainly true.

"You know what I think?" Chuck asked.

"What?"

"I think you're going to end up liking this guy Feinberg. I think you're going to end up getting A's from him, too. Just show him your true stuff, *your* stuff, not your parents', and you'll have it made."

It sounded so easy when Chuck said it. But Cally didn't know if she'd ever be able to make Mr. Feinberg like her.

The toddlers began arriving at two o'clock on Saturday, as Chuck was hanging the last crepe-paper streamers in the Lippincotts' dining room. Mrs. Lippincott had decided that the twenty-dollar fee included helping with the party arrangements beforehand and making sure the festivities got off to a smooth start. Then, after the cake and ice cream had been served, the clowns could slip away to don their costumes. All week long Cally had struggled to keep the practice sessions secret from Steven, so that when she appeared in full clown regalia it would be a complete surprise.

Cally wasn't used to seeing a whole roomful of two-year-olds. They were so small! So small and so noisy and so selfish. Steven and his best friend, Amy, greeted each other with their usual screaming contest, taking turns uttering piercing shrieks and then leaping about like banshees. Megan and Scott at once became engaged in a savage tussle over the same plastic popcorn popper. Cally's father hurriedly produced a duplicate popper, to no avail. Only the original popper would do, and when Megan was pried away from it she joined her tortured screams to Steven's and Amy's happy ones. Rachel amused herself by dragging copper pot covers from an unguarded kitchen cabinet and banging them together in cymbal fashion. Jason clung to his parents and wailed continuously.

"Let's have some *cake* and *ice cream*," Mr. Lippincott called over the din, hoping the magic words would have the desired calming effect. Six two-year-olds stampeded to the table, with their harried parents in tow.

"Can you sing 'Happy Birthday' to Steven?" Mrs. Lippincott asked in an encouraging voice.

She led them in a discordant sing-song of "Happy Birthday," Steven's voice rising above the rest.

The devouring of the cake and ice cream took about five minutes, and it was time for presents. Problems arose immediately. The guests didn't want to surrender their prettily wrapped packages to the birthday boy.

"Mine!" Amy shouted, clutching hers tightly.

"Mine!" the chorus went up. "Mine!"

Nor were the small guests more willing to relinquish the presents once they were unwrapped. Megan clung to her plastic lawnmower, sobbing.

"Yours is at home," her parents tried to explain. "This one is for Steven."

"No!"

"Don't you want to give something nice to Steven? Isn't he your friend?"

"No!"

Mrs. Lippincott gave Cally the signal. Although only twenty minutes of the party had gone by, it was clearly time for a diversion.

Since it was still so hard to manage stairs on her crutches,

Cally changed in the den while Chuck changed in the bathroom down the hall. They shared the big bathroom mirror as they applied their makeup. Stroke by stroke they watched themselves change from ordinary sixth-graders into strange, white-faced individuals with huge, bulbous red noses and gigantic fixed grins. The shocking-orange fright wigs completed the transformation.

"My hands are shaking," Cally whispered when they were done.

"Look," Chuck said. "All we have to do is go out there and have fun and *they'll* have fun. Everybody loves a clown, right? Think about Danny DeMotto. Think about Ronald McDonald. Think about that great clown duo, Chuck Foster and Cally Lippincott!"

Cally started to say something and stopped. What she had started to say was, I *don't love clowns. I've never even* liked *clowns*. But if she hadn't said anything all along, now was not the time to begin.

"What if I forget to honk after the jokes?" she asked. "What if they forget to *laugh* after the jokes?"

Chuck slung the sack of joke props over his shoulder. "You won't and they won't."

Cally hoped he was right.

Mr. Lippincott had herded the party guests into the living room to await the grand entrance of the clowns. From down the hall, Cally sounded an opening fanfare on her kazoo. It came out like a feeble squawk, so she blew it again: da-da-da-DAH! Then they burst in upon the party.

Cally had hoped to be greeted by laughter. In her worst fears she had imagined being greeted by silence. But she had never expected the screams.

74

Steven's was the first and loudest, and, as if on cue, the others joined in. It was immediately obvious that these were not screams of childish delight.

Stricken, Cally rushed over to her little brother. "Steven, it's me, Cally!"

At the sound of her voice, Steven stopped screaming for an instant, but when he caught sight again of Cally's garishly made-up clown face, the screams began anew.

"Look, Steven, here's my cast and my crutches. That proves it's me!"

The screams rose louder.

"Do you see the *funny clowns*?" Mrs. Lippincott asked, raising her voice to be heard over the melee and confusion. Her big smile looked as painted on as Cally's. "These funny clowns are here to make you *laugh*!" She motioned despairingly to Cally. "*Do* something!" she said.

Chuck sprang into action. Quickly he drew a banana peel from his sack, tossed it on the floor, slipped on it, and went sprawling. A few of the parents chuckled. Up he scrambled, only to slip on it a second time, and then a third.

A couple of the toddlers forgot their screams and watched, tears rolling down their cheeks. Cally, giving up on soothing Steven, remembered to honk.

It was time for another gag. Chuck reached into his sack again and produced the huge plastic rose. He pretended to smell it, taking deep rapturous whiffs and rolling his eyes in ecstasy. Then he offered it to Cally. Just as she stooped down to bury her nose in its petals, *zap!* A stream of water squirted her full in the face.

As they had practiced, Cally screamed. And six toddlers who had momentarily fallen silent screamed with her.

Maybe a joke would help? Chuck tapped Cally on the shoulder. "Last night I dreamed I ate a ten-pound marshmallow," he said. No one heard him, so he tried again. "*Last night I dreamed I ate a ten-pound marshmallow!*"

"*So?*" Cally shouted in return.

"*So when I woke up this morning my pillow was gone!*"

Cally honked. No one laughed.

Into the bag of tricks again, Chuck came out with the rubber baseball bat. Balancing on one crutch, Cally tossed him an imaginary baseball, and he pretended to swing at it. Strike one! Chuck stomped up and down, feigning anger, and Cally rubbed her hands in glee. She warmed up for the second pitch. Strike two! This time Chuck shook his fist at Cally and she thumbed her nose at him.

The children were quiet now. Cally's third warm-up was the most elaborate of all, and then the third imaginary baseball went soaring. Chuck swung. Strike three! Cally crowed with triumph, not seeming to notice Chuck sneaking up behind her with the bat.

Boing!

Chuck bopped her on the head and bent double guffawing. Cally closed her eyes and slumped down on her crutches, pretending to be knocked unconscious. She steeled herself for more screams or leaden silence.

Instead she heard the magical sound of children's laughter. They were laughing! They thought the clowns were funny! Rent-a-Clown was going to make it.

Fluttering her eyelids open for a second, Cally saw Rachel sneaking up on Jason with one of the copper pot lids.

Boing!

It was the parents who were screaming now.

Chapter 9

Rachel's parents apologized over and over again to Jason's, as everyone hovered around him anxiously, but Cally's apologized even more. "It was all my fault," Mrs. Lippincott said, near tears. "The clowns were a dreadful mistake."

Jason didn't seem to have a concussion, but his parents decided it was best to take him to the hospital, anyway, to make sure he was all right. Rachel's parents followed a car behind. When the last guests had gone, Cally's parents, too, joined the procession to Maplewood Medical Center.

"It's the least we can do," Cally's mother said. "Margaret, be a dear and look after Steven while we're gone, will you?"

To Chuck she said coldly, "I think you had better run along home, young man."

Even Chuck didn't have the nerve to ask, *What about our twenty dollars?* Still in their clown suits, he and Cally walked his battered bicycle down the driveway.

"I don't get it," Chuck said, clenching his fist as if he wanted to hit himself over the head with it. "I just don't get it. I mean, how could they not like clowns?"

"A lot of people don't like clowns," Cally snapped, near tears. "I don't like clowns. I hate clowns."

Chuck stared at her in disbelief.

"I do. I hate them. I hate everything about them. I've always hated them. They have big fake-grinning mouths, and horrible big red noses, and they think they're so funny, but I think the tricks they play on each other are really mean and stupid."

"But you never said anything—"

"I tried to. But you're like a steamroller. Once you start steaming and rolling, that's it and nobody else can get a word in edgewise. You get one of your brilliant ideas, and that's all that matters. You never stop to ask anybody else if they think it's a good idea. You just assume they'll go along. I never told you I'd sell newspapers with you. I never told you I wanted to do Rent-a-Clown. You make all the plans and you just expect me to follow."

"I didn't know you felt that way," Chuck said in a strangled voice. "I thought it was fun for you, too."

It *was* fun, part of Cally wanted to say. But she knew if she said anything else her voice would break.

"Well, I guess you won't have to worry about any more of my dumb ideas," Chuck said finally. "I guess we're not going to be going to Ocean City, anyway."

Under the garish makeup, he looked more discouraged than she had ever seen him. He looked defeated. Cally watched as he rode away and knew that there is no sadder sight than a heartbroken clown pedaling into the distance on a too-small bicycle.

Her parents had left by the time she returned. Margaret was zipping Steven into his jacket.

"I wish I were dead," Cally said.

"Be patient and your wish will be granted," Margaret told her. Then she gave Cally a hug. "Every kid has to go to an emergency room sometime. It's a law of nature. He'll be all right."

"I got a D in social studies on Thursday."

Margaret looked as if she couldn't see the connection between the two tragedies.

"Every kid has to get a D sometime, too," she said. "Another law of nature. You want to come with us? We're not going far."

Cally shook her head. The only thing she wanted, besides being dead, was to wash off every last speck of greasepaint, fling herself face down on the couch, and pretend the whole afternoon—the whole week? her whole life?—had never happened.

She felt a little better, but not much, when she had changed herself from a clown back to her ordinary Cally self. She scrubbed her face till her cheeks were fiery and tossed the polka-dotted clown costume in a tangled heap on the bedroom floor. Even though it was three in the afternoon, she put on her nightgown and soft terrycloth robe. She lay on the couch now, trying not to notice the party streamers still festively twirled around the banisters.

The party had been a disaster. Rent-a-Clown had been a disaster. But that wasn't what bothered Cally the most. Ten minutes ago she had blamed everything on Chuck. But now she wasn't sure that the disaster hadn't been her fault as much as his.

Cally buried her face deeper in the heap of sofa pillows. She had accused Chuck of assuming that he'd make the plans and she'd follow them, of assuming that whatever grand scheme he cooked up, she'd go along. But a deeper truth, with painful persistence, squirmed its way into view. Chuck

79

assumed that Cally would go along because Cally always *did* go along. Cally had done everything Chuck expected of her, because she always did what people expected of her. She tried to meet everybody's expectations, except for her own.

Cally hadn't even objected when her parents picked aerodynamics engineering for her career project. Why couldn't she have asked to do her report on a career in music? She loved her piano lessons. It would have been fun to interview Mrs. Randolph and read books about famous musicians. Cally could have written an A essay on "A Day in the Life of a Pianist." It was her career, after all, not her parents', and it should have been her career report, too. She had agreed to aerodynamics engineering because she had been afraid of disappointing her parents. But she had ended up disappointing herself—and could imagine how disappointed her parents would be when they found out about her D. She had sat silently when Ashley bragged, not wanting to make Ashley mad. Instead, she had wound up letting Heather get hurt. Both times she had only wanted to go along with what other people wanted, but both times it had backfired.

Her whole problem with Mr. Feinberg was that he was one teacher who didn't want kids telling him what they thought he wanted to hear. He wanted them to have their own opinions. "You do have opinions, don't you?" Mr. Feinberg had asked. But Cally had been so afraid that she might have the wrong opinion that she hadn't let herself have any opinions at all. She hadn't even tried to have opinions of her own; she had been too busy trying to second-guess what Mr. Feinberg wanted. And that was exactly what Mr. Feinberg *didn't* want.

But Cally had certainly gone along with everything Chuck wanted. From the minute he had knocked on her door two and a half weeks ago, she had followed his lead on everything. She had said what he wanted her to say and done what he wanted her to do. And now they had lost the *County Times* contest, anyway, and sent Jason to the hospital emergency room.

The funny thing was that Cally wouldn't have figured out any of this if it hadn't been for Chuck. He was the one who had shown her how exciting life can be when you have some dreams of your own, dreams that you're willing to go out on a limb for. Even if he went too far in the other direction, even if they had lost the *County Times* contest and failed with Rent-a-Clown, she didn't want to give up her friendship with Chuck. She didn't want her life to be the way it had been before.

What would be the worst thing that could happen if she didn't go along—if she took a chance, staked out an idea of her own and acted on it? Well, sometimes she'd say or do something that she'd be sorry for. But she could hardly be any sorrier than she was now.

"We're home!" her father called from the front hall.

"Are you feeling all right, sweetie pie?" her mother asked, coming into the living room and seeing Cally on the couch in her nightgown and robe.

"Just tired," Cally said. She sat up hopefully. Her mother wouldn't have called her "sweetie pie" if Jason was in any danger.

"Good news," her father said. "Jason's going to be all right. The doctor told his parents to keep an eye on him for a couple of days, but they don't think it's a concussion, just a nasty bump."

Cally's heart soared with relief.

"It wasn't really your fault, honey," Mr. Lippincott said.

"Children that age need to be watched every minute."

"Still," Cally said, "Chuck and I should have planned the program better. In fact, I think kids Steven's age are too young for clowns. I should have helped Chuck think of something else."

"I must say, you're taking a very mature attitude," her father said, obviously pleased.

"Speaking of Chuck," Cally's mother said, "I'm not sure this compromise of your father's is working out. We agreed that you could have three afternoons a week to use as you please until your cast comes off, but maybe it's time to reconsider. I think your time would be better spent, honey, on catching up in those math and science review books. Or maybe you could sit in on ballet and gymnastics as an observer, so you won't feel so behind when your cast comes off."

Cally took a deep breath. "I—well, I don't want to do ballet and gymnastics anymore."

"Of course you do," Mrs. Lippincott began, but Cally plunged ahead before she lost her nerve.

"No, I don't. I mean, I really don't. I don't want to sit in on them now, and I don't want to do them when my cast comes off."

"You're just afraid you won't catch up, but, believe me, before you know it you'll be right back up with the others."

"But I don't want to," Cally repeated desperately. She didn't know how to explain. "I want to have some, you know, free time, time just for me."

"What would you do with it?" Cally's father asked.

"I want to start a new business with Chuck," Cally surprised herself by saying. "I know Rent-a-Clown didn't work out, but I think we learned a lot from doing it." She had to admit, "It was the most fun I've ever had in my life."

"Oh, Cally." Cally's mother packed so much disappointment into the two short words that it was all Cally could do not to take back everything she had said and vow to become simultaneously a world-champion gymnast and prima ballerina.

"Cally, life's not just about having fun," Mrs. Lippincott said slowly. "If all you do is have fun now, where will you be when you're seventeen and applying for college? What are you going to write on your college applications? 'I had fun'? Your father and I want to give you a good start now, so you'll have a shot in a few years at the best colleges, so you can have the profession of your choice when you're grown up. Do you think the two of us sit around having fun all the time? We don't. But we love our work, and we love our lives. We wouldn't trade what we do for a few hours of clowning."

"It's not just having fun." Cally tried again. "It's that—well, I want to do something that's mine. Something that I think up all by myself. You know, where I plan it and I really think hard about how to make it all work out. And even if I fail at it, it'll be something I failed at."

"But when you do these—these *things* with Chuck, it seems to me that he leads and you follow."

Her mother had her there. "That's how it was," Cally admitted. "But that's not how it's going to be. And in other things, too. Like my school papers. Like my career report. I want to think up what I want to do them on. I want to do them myself."

"All parents help their children. We take an interest in your work because we care."

"Mr. Feinberg wouldn't even grade our career reports

83

because he said our parents had done them. He made us write an essay instead, right in class, on a day in the life of our career person. And when I did mine, all I could remember was something about wind tunnels and viscous fluids and I got a—bad grade."

Mrs. Lippincott looked troubled. "What did you get?"

It would be easier to tell her parents that she had murdered somebody. At least her father had experience with confessions like that.

"I got a D."

"That's ridiculous." Cally could tell her mother was angry now. "I'm going to call your teacher and arrange for a conference. You're not a D student. He'll have to change that grade."

"It wasn't Mr. Feinberg's fault," Cally said. "Please don't call him. My essay was horrible. It really was."

"Maybe we've been pushing you too hard," Cally's father said, since her mother was too upset to go on. "I think your Mr. Feinberg is probably right that a lot of parents today are helping with homework more than they should. If we're not helping you in the end to be able to think for yourself, then we shouldn't be doing it. It looks like maybe we've made some mistakes.

"But let's get back to your after-school activities. You've spent a lot of years working up to where you are now in ballet and gymnastics. Are you going to look back someday and be sorry that you didn't keep going?"

Cally thought hard about the question. "Maybe. But I don't think so. I mean, I'll still do the piano. I can practice a lot more if I have more free time. And I'll bring my math and science grades up, I promise. It's just that, well, I think I'd be more sorry someday if I hadn't done the things I wanted to do. If I hadn't even figured out the things I wanted to do."

"It's up to you, Cally," Mrs. Lippincott said with some difficulty, putting her arm around Cally's shoulders. "We've only wanted what we thought was best for you."

"Then I don't have to do gymnastics and ballet?"

"You don't have to do gymnastics and ballet," Mr. Lippincott said. "But let me make one suggestion. My suggestion is that you and Chuck swear off clowning for a while. What do you say?"

With the tension broken, Cally laughed, and her mother, a little shakily at first, joined in.

"Don't worry," Cally promised joyfully. "My clowning career is officially over."

Chapter 10

Sunday morning Cally stayed in bed late, a notebook propped up on her bent knees, working on a plan. She laid it out in perfect outline form, which would have gladdened her fifth-grade teacher's heart. Mr. Nelson had had an obsession with outline form. Across the top of the page she wrote: Entertainment Enterprises (Formerly Known as Rent-a-Clown). Then she read over what she had written from top to bottom.

Entertainment Enterprises
(Formerly Known as Rent-a-Clown)

I. Purpose
    A. To help mothers with kids' birthday parties
        1. Ages 3–10 only
        2. No two-year-olds
    B. To earn $200 for the Fosters and Cally to go to Ocean City
II. Services provided
    A. Decorations
        1. Hanging crepe-paper streamers from ceiling fixtures
        2. Twining crepe-paper streamers around banisters
        3. Tying crepe-paper bows for use where needed

B. Refreshments
1. Will be provided by the parents
2. But we'll help serve
3. And clean up crumbs and spills

C. Entertainment
1. Party games
   a. Pin the Tail on the Donkey
   b. Musical Chairs
   c. Madlibs
   d. Others
2. Magic tricks
   a. Plucking coins from thin air
   b. Card tricks
   c. Pulling rabbits out of a hat
   d. Others
3. Absolutely no clowning whatsoever

III. Fee
A. $20
B. Plus tips

Cally sighed with pleasure when she finished reading it. She was grateful to Mr. Nelson for his thorough drilling in outline form.

For breakfast Cally's father made french toast, a Lippincott family Sunday morning tradition. Then Cally waited impatiently for Chuck's family to return home from Sunday school and church. Cally's family didn't go to church, except on Christmas Eve and Easter, but Chuck's family went faithfully every Sunday. Church lasted from eleven to twelve, Cally knew.

At five past twelve she dialed his number and tried again at five-minute intervals after that. At twelve twenty-five Chuck finally answered.

"I have a plan, the most wonderful plan!" she told him.

Chuck seemed bewildered. "I thought you were mad at me."

"Well, I was mad yesterday, but then I thought, well, Rent-a-Clown was my fault, too. If I didn't like clowns, I should have helped us to think of something else. I didn't have to go along with everything. So do you want to hear my new plan?"

"Does it have to do with clowning?" Chuck asked glumly.

"No, it says right in the plan 'Absolutely no clowning whatsoever.' So can you come over this afternoon?"

"Over there?"

Of course over here, Cally was about to say. Then she realized Chuck was dreading a return to the scene of the—not crime, exactly, but miserable failure.

"Or I'll come over to your house," Cally suggested. "Margaret will drive me."

"Okay," Chuck said, without enthusiasm. But that was all right. He hadn't seen the plan yet.

Even after Chuck had seen the plan Cally wasn't sure he liked it. It took him a long time to read it through, as they sat together on the Fosters' front stoop.

"Don't you think we should just give up?" he asked finally.

"You mean, give up on birthday parties? I know the first one was pretty horrible, but at least now we know what *not* to do."

"I mean, give up on the whole Ocean City thing. It seems like every time I get excited about something, I go too far and things get out of control and somebody gets hurt."

"Yes, but—" Cally didn't know what to say. It was true Chuck had a habit of going too far, and going off cockeyed in the wrong direction, but the answer wasn't to give up. It was to keep the train chugging, but keep it under control, keep it on the right track.

"No," she said. "I don't think we should give up. I think we should give Entertainment Enterprises a try. The world *needs* Entertainment Enterprises. At Steven's party *we* needed Entertainment Enterprises."

She giggled, and, reluctantly, Chuck grinned, too.

He looked at the plan again. "Do you know how to pluck coins out of thin air?"

"There're tons of magic books in the library. Probably books on party decorations, too. And party favors."

Chuck got a dreamy look in his eyes. "Parties for all occasions," he said. "Birthdays! Bar mitzvahs! Weddings! Funerals!"

"Not *funerals*!"

This time Cally's objection registered. "You're right," Chuck said, surprised. "You're absolutely right. We don't want to do parties at funerals. We want to do—"

"Birthday parties. For children ages three to ten."

"Right!" Chuck jumped up from the stoop and gave a hand to Cally. "My dad can do terrific card tricks. We'll get him to show us how."

Dum, dum, dum, *dum*, dum, dum, *dum*, dum, dum. Low, mournful notes rose in a stately progression, resonating in the Lippincotts' living room. Cally was practicing the first movement of Beethoven's *Moonlight* Sonata.

It was a beautiful piece of music, at least when someone

else was playing it. Cally had heard it for the first time on the radio a few days after Steven's birthday party, and she had wanted to cry for the sheer beauty of it. She had talked about nothing else at her Friday piano lesson. Mrs. Randolph hadn't been sure that Cally was ready for such a difficult piece, but she had given her the sheet music, anyway, and told her she could try the first movement. It was the first time Cally had ever picked her own piece of music, instead of working through the assigned pieces in the graded piano course books.

Now, on Sunday, Cally felt like crying from frustration. The first few lines were all right, especially since she had practiced them ten thousand times. But next came a long climb up and down the keyboard, crammed full of accidental sharps. Cally always had to give up on it halfway through, which spoiled the mood of the sonata considerably. Taking a deep breath, she plunged once more into the agonizing ascent. Nope. She hit one wrong note and then another.

Mrs. Randolph wouldn't think any less of her if she gave up on the *Moonlight* Sonata for another year or two. But Cally wasn't ready to give up yet. She had chosen the *Moonlight* Sonata as the one piece that she wanted to play most in all the world. *Dum*, dum, dum, *dum*, dum, dum, *dum*, dum, dum. She started all over again at the beginning.

Besides, hard as the *Moonlight* Sonata was, everything else in Cally's life was harder. Entertainment Enterprises, now a week old, was off to a slow start. They hadn't gotten a single call yet, though they had spent Saturday afternoon plastering fliers on every windshield in the Westmark Mall parking lot. Cally's foot still ached from the exertion.

It was just as well that business was slow, since magic tricks required more practice than plain old clowning. Chuck had become pretty good at pulling coins out of thin air, but when Cally tried you could see the edge of the coin poking out between her clenched fingers. Mr. Foster's card tricks were as clever as Chuck had promised, but Cally would forget how to do them halfway through. She hadn't fooled Margaret with a card trick yet.

School was even worse. Mr. Feinberg had assigned the big project for the economics unit, an in-depth report on some business or company. This time, Mr. Feinberg said, there was to be no parental assistance at all. None. He sent notes home to all the parents explaining as much. Ashley's parents would probably cheat and do hers for her, anyway, but Cally's were abiding by the new rule. Her mother hadn't so much as asked her what her report was going to be about, although Cally knew she was dying to know.

The problem was that Cally didn't know herself. Ashley was doing hers on Apple Computers. When she found this out, Heather, who had planned to do hers on Apple Computers, too, quickly changed to IBM. Justin had chosen McDonald's, which would have been fun if Cally had thought of it first. But now it would be copying to pick Roy Rogers or Burger King. There were millions of magazine articles on Apple, IBM, and McDonald's. The others could hardly help getting A's. Of course, Mr. Feinberg didn't want them just to repeat everything some magazine had said. He wanted their own ideas.

Cally was halfway through the long climb when she got stuck again. She couldn't concentrate on the *Moonlight* Sonata when she was so worried about her social studies project. She would have to get an A+ on her economics report to make up for the D on "A Day in the Life of an Aerodynamics Engineer." Resolutely, Cally forced that thought from her mind and focused sternly on Beethoven.

Dum, dum, dum, *dum*, dum, dum . . .

The doorbell rang in time to save Cally from another defeat. Cally's parents were out at their Sunday afternoon chamber music concert series, so Cally kept the chain on when she opened the front door. But it was Chuck, grinning as broadly as he had the day she'd met him. He was carrying a large cardboard carton with what looked like air holes punched in the sides.

Inside the carton something thumped.

Cally let Chuck in, but didn't take the carton from him. She had a horrible feeling there was something *alive* in there, like an animal.

"Does your father have a black silk top hat?" Chuck asked. "Because if he's got the hat, I've got the rabbit!"

"A real live rabbit?"

Chuck looked insulted. "Do you think Entertainment Enterprises would pull a *dead* rabbit out of a hat?"

He set the carton on the piano bench and gently lifted off the lid. Nestled in a pile of shredded *County Times* papers was a small, brown baby rabbit that no one could be afraid of.

"Ohh," she said.

"You can pet her, if you like."

Timidly Cally put out a finger and stroked the bunny's soft fur.

"I don't have a hat, though," she said. "Besides, we need a

special kind of hat, with a fake bottom for hiding rabbits in."

"I'll try to get one at Merlin's House of Magic tomorrow so we can start practicing right away."

"What's the big hurry?" Cally asked, stroking the bunny again, this time with her whole hand.

"Didn't I tell you? We have our first party lined up! Next Saturday, from two to four. The lady called me as I was heading out the door."

Cally hugged him.

"Come on," she said. "Let's practice that one card trick again, okay? You know, the one where I smell the cards?"

Chapter 11

On Monday Ashley bragged so much at lunchtime that Cally decided she must have a disease: bragitis. Cally couldn't help hoping that in advanced stages bragitis would prove fatal. First the victim brags incessantly for a few years, then before you know it, she drops dead. The prospect was undeniably satisfying. It was hard to feel sorry for someone who had bragged herself to death.

If bragitis didn't kill Ashley, the other sixth-grade girls very well might. But short of murder, it wasn't clear what to do about somebody with bragitis. Everything the girls tried only made the bragging worse.

Cally usually tried changing the subject, but there didn't seem to be a subject Ashley couldn't brag about. Bicycles, ice cream, TV shows—Ashley could brag about them all. If you had a ten-speed bike, she had a twelve-speed. Whatever brand of ice cream you liked, she liked some kind that was more expensive. Her cousin out in California had dated the stars of every TV show ever made and was going to introduce them all to Ashley the next time she visited.

Another strategy was to try bragging back, but a bragging race with Ashley escalated faster than an arms race with the Russians.

"My father had lunch with the governor yesterday," Ashley once said.

Cally hadn't been able to resist. "My father had lunch with the Hillside ax murderer."

That had been the only time anyone had emerged victorious from a bragging match with Ashley. If only Ashley would fall off the balance beam again at the next gymnastics meet! Or disgrace herself somehow in ballet.

As part of her new campaign to take charge, Cally had decided to say straight out, "You know, Ashley, we're all pretty tired of hearing you brag." But when she opened her mouth a couple of times to say it, the words wouldn't come out. Deciding to speak up was one thing; doing it was a lot harder.

She asked her parents about it at dinner on Monday night. Steven was upstairs with Margaret, so they didn't have to dodge any flying beets or potatoes.

"What would you do if you had a friend who bragged all the time?" A father who had lunch with murderers and a mother who might win a Nobel Prize in economics should be able to think of something.

"I'd tell her," Mrs. Lippincott said promptly. That was what Cally had been afraid she would say. "I'd tell her how you feel about the bragging. You can do it nicely. Tell her that it makes the rest of you feel bad. Tell her that she doesn't need to brag, that you'd still like her, anyway."

"But no one likes her," Cally protested.

"It's called a little white lie," her father said. "You're not testifying under oath. It doesn't have to be the truth, the whole truth, and nothing but the truth."

"What if she gets mad?"

"Then she gets mad," Mrs. Lippincott said. "It doesn't sound like the end of the world to me."

Cally sighed. The speakers-up of the world certainly had a lot of terrible things to look forward to.

She knew without asking anyone that it was only fair to talk to Ashley alone, without an audience. The next day, before she could talk herself out of it, she followed Ashley into the girls' room before lunch.

"I like your sweater," Cally said awkwardly. She didn't know how she'd ever get to the subject of bragging.

But Ashley made it easy for her. "It cost thirty-five dollars," Ashley said. "It's a hundred percent pure wool. Yours is acrylic, isn't it?"

Cally took a deep breath. "Ashley?" she began, and stopped.

"Uh-huh?"

"Ashley, there's something— Well, I don't really know how to say this, but—"

Hardly looking at Cally, Ashley brushed a bit of lint off her sleeve.

"You see"—it was now or never—"the rest of us, well, it's hard for us when you brag so much."

Now Ashley looked at Cally. Her cheeks flamed.

"It's just that—it makes us feel bad. Heather, especially. She still minds about Camp Danforth and all, and you keep rubbing it in. Or the part in the ballet."

"I don't think I brag," Ashley said stiffly. "I mean, I have to talk about *something*. I can't help it if I get everything and Heather doesn't."

Cally didn't retreat. "We all like *you*, Ashley." The small white lie loomed large and preposterous. "We just can't take the bragging."

"Well, excu-u-u-se me!" Ashley said, with all the dignity she could muster. Holding her head high, she swept out of the girls' room.

Cally's hands were still trembling as she carried her tray through the cafeteria line. What should she do when she saw Ashley again? Say she was sorry? She wasn't sorry.

But when Ashley slid into place at their table, she looked as if nothing had happened. She smiled and laughed as always. Except not quite as always.

"I love your sweater, Ashley," Heather said. "It's beautiful." Cally's fork was poised in midair.

"Thank you," Ashley said awkwardly. She hesitated, and then added, half under her breath, "Yours is pretty, too."

And right then, Cally *did* like Ashley, after all. Heather flashed Cally a look that said, *What is going on here?* Smiling serenely, Cally kept on eating.

Two days before the party, Cally could produce coins out of thin air as if she'd been doing it all her life. At lunch she plucked a dime from Heather's ear and a quarter from Ashley's. (Ashley didn't brag that her coin was bigger.)

Under her friends' admiring gaze, Cally then pulled out a well-thumbed pack of playing cards from her book bag. She shuffled them as deftly as she could and fanned out the cards, face down, in a smooth semicircle.

"Here," she told Heather. "Pick a card, any card. Look at it, but don't tell me what it is."

Heather obeyed.

"Okay, put it back." Cally cut the deck for her, just happening to notice that the bottom card, the card that would fall right before Heather's, was the seven of spades.

She cut the deck a few more times so that Heather's card would be well hidden in it. Then one by one she worked her way through the pack, sniffing each card in turn. "Nope. Nope. Not this one, either." Only after she had made her pronouncement did she glance casually at each rejected card.

She pretended to smell one card more closely, as if it might bear the telltale odor. "No," she said, with some apparent hesitation. "No, this isn't it."

A third of the way through, she saw that the last card sniffed and rejected was the seven of spades. Since however often she had cut the deck, the order of the cards stayed the same, this meant that Heather's card was the very next one. Cally picked it up and inhaled luxuriously.

"Mmm," she said, breathing deeply. "*This* is your card!"

With a flourish she turned over the jack of hearts and waited for Heather's reaction.

"How did you *do* that?" Heather asked.

Cally tapped her nose. "I've always had a good sense of smell," she said.

"No, tell us how you really did it," Ashley protested.

"Magic," Cally said airily, and the bell rang.

But it was going to take more than magic to produce out of thin air a topic for her economics project for Mr. Feinberg. This was the day the sixth-grade social studies students were supposed to have their topics ready to tell the class. Cally had spent half the weekend trying to think of what hers should be, but she still couldn't find one that seemed wonderful enough to make up for "A Day in the Life of an Aerodynamics Engineer."

She had decided she didn't want to do a report like Heather's and Ashley's, where all you did was copy out of a million magazine articles, changing the words a little bit so it wouldn't really count as copying. Instead she wanted to pick a local business where she could do first-hand research, as if she were a real reporter for a newspaper or magazine. But it was hard to find a local business that would be just right.

Reliable Dry Cleaning? Too boring. Sally's Sweet Shoppe? Maybe. Cally liked their hand-dipped chocolates, but the manager was mean and didn't like kids. The best idea she had come up with was the *County Times*. At least she knew all the important things already: pennies a day, most classified ads, high school sports scores, delivered in all weather. But her parents would have to drive her to the newspaper's offices in Rockville, and she didn't want to ask for any help from her parents. And it wasn't *special* enough.

"Okay, class," Mr. Feinberg said, when they were all seated and the bell had rung. "Let's go around the room and hear your project topics. Let's see what you folks could come up with on your own."

One by one, each student reported his or her choice. IBM; Apple; McDonald's; Ringling Brothers, Barnum & Bailey circus; Haägen-Dazs Ice Cream; Walt Disney World. As Cally's turn drew closer, her heart raced and she could feel her cheeks burning with nervous dread. She wished she could think of a business no one else could even imagine writing about, a completely original project that only she could do.

Suddenly the idea came to her. She couldn't believe she hadn't thought of it sooner. Mr. Feinberg hadn't said the report had to be on a *big* business or company.

"Cally?" Mr. Feinberg asked. "What did you pick?"

She took a deep breath. "Entertainment Enterprises."

Mr. Feinberg looked puzzled. "I don't believe I'm familiar with that company. Can you tell us a little more about it?"

Everyone was looking at her now. Maybe Mr. Feinberg would think it was cheating to do a report on her own business. And Entertainment Enterprises didn't look like much of a business compared to Apple Computers or IBM.

"It's—well, it's my own business," she stammered. "I'm one of the two co-owners." Her mind seized on the outline she had made for Chuck. "We provide assistance at birthday parties for children ages three to ten. We help with decorations and refreshments and also offer a program of entertainment."

"What kind of entertainment? Party games? Clowning?"

"We decided against clowning," Cally said. "We tried that in an earlier business, called Rent-a-Clown, but it didn't work out. In fact, my report will give the reasons that Rent-a-Clown failed."

Mr. Feinberg didn't say anything, so Cally went on. "I'll also give an account of how much we spend and how much we earn and tell how and where we advertise. It'll be sort of an up-to-date progress report on our successes so far, because it's a new company and we're just starting."

That was all Cally had to say. She was afraid to see the expression on Mr. Feinberg's face. Would he say something sarcastic? *You call that a company? You call that a paper topic?*

"Splendid!" Mr. Feinberg said. Cally forced herself to look up. He was smiling broadly. "Frankly, I can't think of a topic that sounds more interesting. I was counting on you kids to come up with some pretty terrific ideas once you were on your own, and you haven't let me down. I'll be looking forward to your report, Cally. It sounds like a winner."

Mr. Feinberg turned to the next student. "What about you, Scott?"

"Well, my idea's nothing super-original like Cally's, but . . ."

Yes, it really was turning out to be a most satisfactory day!

Chuck was supposed to come by directly from school, at three-thirty. Cally practiced the first movement of the *Moonlight* Sonata while she waited. Once she almost made it through, but her fingers were so used to failing that, almost out of habit, they stumbled just before she reached the end. *Dum*, dum, dum . . . She practiced harder than she ever had before.

When she glanced at her watch, Cally was surprised to see that it was past four o'clock already. Chuck was late. Maybe he had forgotten it was Thursday, but Cally had never known Chuck to forget anything. Where could he be? Cally had a sudden mischievous hunch: detention! Chuck had told her that he was going to try to smuggle Abby the Rabbit (short for Abracadabra) into school one day.

Cally heard someone at the front door. It was her mother.

"Hi, sweetie pie. Where's Chuck?"

"I don't know," Cally said, puzzled. "He didn't come."

"Maybe he had homework to do. Even Chuck does homework sometimes, I imagine."

Cally glared at her mother. "For your information, Chuck

is a very good student." Mr. Foster thought so much of education that his children would never let themselves fall behind. "But he wouldn't stay home just to do homework."

The phone rang, and Cally ran to get it. It wasn't Chuck; it was some raspy-voiced person.

"Hi, Cally," the person said. "I can't come over today."

It *was* Chuck!

"You sound terrible," Cally told him. "Are you sick?"

"Can you believe it? I have the flu. I told my mom that I felt well enough to ride over to your house this afternoon, but she said if I'm too sick to go to school, I'm too sick to go for a bike ride."

Cally could hardly imagine Chuck sick. She would have thought he could fast-talk germs the way he fast-talked *County Times* customers.

"The thing is, the doctor doesn't think I'll be better in time for the weekend."

The weekend! The thought jolted Cally like a bolt of static electricity from the science class experiment. This weekend was the first party for Entertainment Enterprises. Saturday was just two days away.

"But you—you have to be!"

Chuck sounded miserable. "There's no way my mom will let me go. It's like a prison camp here, I mean it. So it's up to you, Cally. Should we cancel the party or can you do it alone? I know you'll have a devil of a time hanging crepe paper with your crutches and all."

For a fleeting moment Cally missed the old Chuck, the bossy Chuck, who would have told her to "go get 'em, tiger" and not taken no for an answer. The thought of canceling the party was wonderfully tempting. She wasn't ready for the first public testing of Entertainment Enterprises. Another few weeks of planning and practice would be all to the good.

If it had been Rent-a-Clown, the decision would be easy. The party would have been canceled as soon as Cally could dial the lady's number. But Entertainment Enterprises was Cally's own brainchild. She dreaded the thought of doing the party all by herself, alone. It lay like a lump of cold, undigested oatmeal in the pit of her stomach. But she had felt the same way about talking to her parents about ballet and gymnastics, about telling Ashley that she bragged too much, about presenting her project topic in Mr. Feinberg's class. All those things had seemed impossible to her, and yet she had done them all.

Cally found her voice. "I'll do it," she said faintly.

"You'll be great!" Chuck assured her jubilantly. "My dad'll bring Abby by your house this evening, okay? I hope your mother likes rabbits. And he'll bring some of the other stuff you'll need, like the magic top hat."

Cally had forgotten about Abby. Already she regretted her rash promise. But what was the worst thing that could happen if the party failed?

"My mom says I have to hang up now. Knock 'em dead, Cally."

Knock 'em dead! It was more likely that they would knock *her* dead.

Chapter 12

At noon on Saturday Cally stood on the front stoop of the party house, steeling herself to ring the doorbell. She was all alone except for Abby the Rabbit, hidden in a cardboard carton at her feet. How could she have dreaded selling *County Times* subscriptions? Each sales pitch had taken less than two minutes, with Chuck only a few steps away, ready to take on any mean man who yelled at her. Here, with preparation and cleanup, the party would last five hours. And this time Chuck was a mile away, home in bed. Cally was completely, utterly, absolutely on her own.

She pressed the button. Moments later, the party mother opened the door. She was a short, stylishly dressed woman, with a sharp-featured face and watchful eyes. If anything went wrong at the party, Mrs. Abramson wouldn't be likely to miss it.

"Where's the boy?" she asked suspiciously.

"He's at home sick. He has the flu."

Mrs. Abramson looked as if she thought Cally was making it up. Her look said, *Why not say he has the Bubonic plague, too, while you're at it?*

"Will you be able to manage on your crutches?" she asked. "Daniel's friends are very *active* children."

The crutches were going to be the least of Cally's problems. "I can manage," she said, remembering, a trifle too late, to flash her Olympic champion smile.

For the next two hours Cally was too busy to be nervous. Mrs. Abramson was apparently determined to get her money's worth from Entertainment Enterprises. First Cally helped decorate chocolate cupcakes. She frosted each one carefully, not licking the knife in between the way she would have at home. Then the frosted cupcakes were crowned with miniature plastic baseballs, bats, and catcher's mitts.

Cally waited for a comment on how pretty the cupcakes looked, but instead Mrs. Abramson led her over to an enormous plastic bag bulging full of green and yellow balloons.

"I have to run to the store," she said. "While I'm gone you can start on these."

Cally's heart sank. She hated blowing up balloons. It was no accident that there had been no mention of balloons on the Entertainment Enterprises outline. She wished Rumpelstiltskin would appear and offer to blow up all the balloons in exchange for her firstborn child. But when after a few minutes he still hadn't appeared, there was nothing for her to do but doggedly start blowing.

Cally blew and blew and blew. Ten balloons done, ninety to go. She looked around for Rumpelstiltskin again and caught sight of Daniel, the party boy, watching her from behind the sofa.

"I can blow up balloons," he said, with just-turned-seven confidence.

Cally thought quickly. Would he blow up more balloons if she said "I bet you can!" or "I bet you can't!"? To be on the safe side, she tried both approaches. "I bet you're a good balloon blower-upper," she said. "But I bet you can't blow up all the balloons in this big, big bag."

"I can, too," Daniel said.

Here you go, kid! Cally handed him the bag, cheered him on for the first few balloons, and then got busy with the crepe paper. She twirled streamers festively around the banisters, the way they had done at Steven's party, and hung crepe-paper bows wherever she could reach. But all alone, with her leg in a heavy cast, Cally couldn't very well scramble on top of furniture to hang streamers from the windows.

Cally eyed Daniel again.

"I can hang streamers," the birthday boy volunteered. "I can climb high!"

"I bet you're a good climber," Cally said. "But I bet you can't climb on top of the bookcase to hang these streamers."

"I can, too!"

Up he went, as easily as on monkey bars at a playground. In a few minutes the living room and dining room were transformed.

Back from her errand, Mrs. Abramson looked in and nodded approvingly. "Very nice."

"I did it!" Daniel crowed.

Mrs. Abramson glanced inquiringly at Cally.

"I let him help," Cally said with a smile. Then she reached over and plucked a shiny new penny from Daniel's ear and handed it to him. He stared at it in wonderment.

"It's real," Cally said. "It's yours."

He looked so thrilled that Cally felt her first stirring of hope. Maybe the party—and the rest of her life—would be all right.

At ten minutes till two the first child arrived, followed by six more. Cally plucked a coin from the ear of each new arrival, and each child clutched his or her penny as an enchanted treasure.

"It's a magic penny," Cally assured each in turn. Then she added, "But the magic only works if you're very, very good." It was worth a try, anyway.

And it seemed to work. Or maybe seven-year-olds were just more manageable than two-year-olds. In any case, Cally had no trouble leading the small guests to the party table. They sang "Happy Birthday" loudly and lustily, and surrendered their presents without a single tantrum. One child spilled his lemonade, but Cally had a sponge handy.

"It's a magic sponge," she said, as she neatly wiped up the sticky puddle. "See, it's all gone! By magic!"

"That's not magic," the lemonade-spiller scoffed. "It's just a plain old sponge."

He had a point there. Cally thought fast. "No, it's magic. Watch." She took her black silk top hat, the one with the fake bottom, from the sideboard. Into it she popped the sponge, then flipped the false bottom so that the sponge was hidden from sight.

"See, it disappeared," she said, letting the children peer, wide-eyed, into the apparently empty hat. Then she reached into the hat, flipped the false bottom again, and made the sponge reappear.

"Ta-dah!" Cally exclaimed triumphantly. The children crowded forward to touch the magic sponge, and the lemonade-spiller was very respectful after that.

When the cupcakes and ice cream had been devoured and the presents opened, Cally led the children into the living room. She plucked a few brightly colored scarves out of thin air—enough for every child to take one home—and produced her deck of playing cards.

"Daniel, you're the birthday boy, so you can go first," Cally said. She shuffled quickly, fanned out the cards, and told him, "Pick a card, any card."

Daniel grabbed the three of hearts and happily held it up for all to see.

"No," Cally said. "*You* look at it, but don't let me see it. Because I have to guess it, okay?"

Daniel nodded solemnly. He picked another card, this time carefully shielding it from Cally's view, and Cally began her great card-smelling trick. It worked for Daniel and his friends as spectacularly as it had for Ashley and Heather. Each child clamored for a turn.

There were eight children at the party, and by the time the eighth child, with agonizing slowness, was choosing her card, Cally could tell the others were becoming restless. Two little girls were climbing up on the couch to yank down crepe-paper streamers. Two little boys were noisily executing one of Daniel's stuffed animals, by firing squad.

"Children!" Mrs. Abramson called sharply. In the nick of time she rescued both the crepe-paper streamers and Tuffles the Bear. "Let Cally finish."

"*This* is your card," Cally told the last little girl wearily. Hardly waiting for the gasp of astonishment, she quickly swept the deck of cards out of sight. She had smelled enough playing cards to last for the rest of her life.

"Now, children, if you're very good, Cally has another magic trick to show you."

Cally wished Mrs. Abramson hadn't said that. She had used up all her magic tricks except one, and the one that was left wasn't guaranteed to be a surefire success like smelling the cards. Cally had a terrible feeling it was guaranteed to be a surefire *failure*. But with eight pairs of eyes looking at her expectantly, there was nothing to do but give it a try.

"Um—I'll be back in a minute." Taking her black silk top hat with her, she hurried out to the kitchen where she had left the cardboard carton with Abracadabra in it. Somehow she was going to have to get the bunny into the magic top hat and out again. She missed Chuck with all her might.

"Okay, Abby, this is your big moment," Cally whispered. Very slowly, she lifted the lid off the carton, afraid Abby would try to escape. She was reassured to find that Abby was curled up in a furry ball, sleeping.

Cally poked the slumbering bunny gently, and Abby opened one eye. *Now what?* Cally didn't know how to talk to a rabbit. *I bet you're good at hiding in hats, but I bet you can't hide in this big, black one!* What if Abby bit her hand? What if Abby bit her hand, *and* it turned out that Abby had rabies, *and* Cally had to have twenty rabies shots in her stomach, *and* Cally died, anyway?

"Don't bite me, Abby," Cally pleaded. Before she lost her nerve, she scooped up the rabbit and plopped her in the bottom of the hat. Then she flipped the false bottom so that Abby was hidden from sight.

With trembling hands Cally carried the black silk top hat back out to the party. She didn't arrive any too soon. Several of the crepe-paper streamers were down, and Tuffles the Bear was in danger of death by decapitation.

"Boys and girls!" Cally cried loudly. The children quieted down enough for her to be heard. "Do you remember my magic hat?"

She strode around the room with it, holding it down low so that the children could inspect its empty interior.

"It's completely empty, right? But you'd be surprised what you can find sometimes in an empty hat. . . ."

She pretended to be groping around in it for unseen treasures.

"She's going to pull out another dumb sponge," the lemonade-spiller predicted.

"This is no dumb sponge!" Cally cried theatrically. In the hushed silence that filled the room now, she reached inside the hat once more and flipped the false bottom.

Cally had a vague memory that TV magicians pulled the rabbit out by its ears, but that seemed too cruel. She hesitated. That split second of hesitation was all Abby needed. No longer asleep, she tore out of the top hat as if she had been shot out of a cannon.

The children laughed and clapped and cheered. Cally was too stunned to scream, but Mrs. Abramson screamed for her, "Get that rabbit out of my house!"

Cally tried to chase Abby, but a girl on crutches is no match for an infuriated rabbit. Delighted by the turn of events, the children joined in the race, shouting with glee. Into the kitchen Abby fled, knocking over the trash can in her headlong flight. A broom propped against the doorjamb crashed into the counter, shattering a teacup.

It was Cally who had the idea of opening the back door. The instant she flung it open, out Abby flew.

"Come back!" the children called after her. "Come back!" But Cally knew that Abby had retired once and for all from show business. She was gone for good.

By then the party was over. The first parents began arriving to collect their children.

"It was the bestest party I was ever at in my whole life!" one child told her parents.

"Can I go to another party tomorrow?" another begged his mother. "Oh, can I? Can I?"

"I've never seen my little girl so excited," the mother of a third remarked to Mrs. Abramson. "That must have been some party!"

"It *was* some party," Mrs. Abramson agreed grimly. But in the face of so much childish rapture she couldn't remain angry. Cally looked over at her anxiously, and Mrs. Abramson gave an unmistakable wink.

Finally all the guests had departed, and Cally, exhausted, began clearing the party table.

"So how did you like your party?" Mrs. Abramson asked Daniel.

"I didn't like it," Daniel said solemnly. Cally's heart caught in her throat. "I *loved* it."

"Oh, just leave those, Cally," Mrs. Abramson said. "I think you've done enough for one day. Maybe more than enough." She laughed and reached for her pocketbook. "I was just going to pay you ten dollars, since the twenty dollars was to have been for two children. But you did the work of two children, and more." She handed Cally a crisp twenty-dollar bill.

Cally thanked Mrs. Abramson and gave Daniel a good-bye hug. "Thanks for all the help, pardner," she whispered. Then she went out front to wait for Margaret. She ached in every muscle, but she was too happy to care. She had thought up Entertainment Enterprises on her own, and she had done the very first party on her own. She was ready now to climb Mount Everest and swim the English Channel and play the *Moonlight* Sonata and say brilliant things in Mr. Feinberg's class.

"I did it!" she shouted to herself, and the words echoed in her heart: *I did it!*

Chapter 13

It was a sunny Saturday afternoon in early May, two weeks after Daniel Abramson's birthday party. Cally's cast had come off the day before. Freed from it, her leg looked like a dead white thing, shriveled and scrawny, but it worked just like a real leg.

"I can't believe we have three more parties lined up," Chuck said, sprawling on a lawn chair in Cally's backyard. "It was great of Mrs. Abramson to recommend us to all her friends. If they like us, too, we'll be all set."

"But I'm a little worried," Cally said, "because nothing as wonderful as Abracadabra's escape can happen at any of the other parties."

"Well, look at it this way. Nothing as terrible can happen, either. We can think of other things to do instead. How about wheelbarrow rides? We could blindfold the kids first and then wheel them all around and they could try to guess where they were."

"Maybe we could play the piano at parties, too. I can play the first movement of the *Moonlight* Sonata now, about a hundred times better than I could before, and you can do 'Ocean City, Here We Come!' "

The two pieces together would make a peculiar musical program, but at least it would offer something for everyone.

Cally hadn't even told Chuck her best news. "Guess what grade I got on my economics report for social studies, the one about Entertainment Enterprises."

"An A," Chuck predicted confidently.

"Wrong."

He looked puzzled.

"A *plus*. So, see, Entertainment Enterprises isn't hurting my grades. It's making them even better."

"We're going to have fun at Ocean City, too," Chuck said. "We can go swimming and look for shells and stuff ourselves all day with crab cakes and Italian ices."

"But then what? I mean, what will we do after that?" Cally asked. In an odd way she wasn't looking forward to the Ocean City trip, because planning for it was more fun than the trip itself could ever be.

"I guess we'll have to earn money for something else then. Maybe there'll be some kid who needs a kidney transplant and we can organize a big campaign to help pay his hospital bills. Or we can buy ourselves a telescope, like your father was talking about, and maybe we *will* discover a planet or a comet or something."

"Maybe I'll teach you how to read music, and we can play duets together and get good enough to put on concerts and win prizes. We'll be a famous two-piano team: Chuck Foster and Cally Lippincott."

"And we can always go to Ocean City next year, too."

Cally hopped up from the chaise lounge, still a little gingerly because of her leg. She led Chuck into the living room. With a flourish, he seated himself at the Lippincotts' piano and then swung into the familiar bouncy tune. Together they sang at the top of their lungs, "Ocean City, Here We Come!"

MEET THE GIRLS FROM CABIN SIX IN <u>CAMP SUNNYSIDE FRIENDS</u>, A GREAT NEW CAMELOT SERIES! THEY'LL BE *YOUR* FRIENDS FOR LIFE!

Their adventures
begin in June 1989.

Look for

CAMP SUNNYSIDE FRIENDS #1
NO BOYS ALLOWED!
75700-1   ($2.50 U.S./$2.95 Canada)
Will the boys at the neighboring camp be asked
to join the all-girl Camp Sunnyside?
Not if the girls in Cabin Six can stop them!

CAMP SUNNYSIDE FRIENDS #2
CABIN SIX PLAYS CUPID
75701-X   ($2.50 U.S./$2.95 Canada)
When their favorite counselor breaks up with her
boyfriend, the girls of Cabin Six hatch a daring
plan to save true love!

HOWLING GOOD FUN
FROM AVON CAMELOT

Meet the 5th graders of P.S. 13—
the craziest, creepiest kids ever!

M IS FOR MONSTER
                    75423-1/$2.75 US/$3.25 CAN
by Mel Gilden; illustrated by John Pierard

BORN TO HOWL   75425-8/$2.50 US/$3.25 CAN
by Mel Gilden; illustrated by John Pierard

THERE'S A BATWING IN MY
        LUNCHBOX   75426-6/$2.75 US/$3.25 CAN
by Ann Hodgman; illustrated by John Pierard

THE PET OF FRANKENSTEIN
        75185-2/$2.50 US/$2.50 US/$3.25 CAN
by Mel Gilden; illustrated by John Pierard

Z IS FOR ZOMBIE 75686-2/$2.75 US/$3.25 CAN
by Mel Gilden; illustrated by John Pierard